All Hands Below

by

Lelani Black

All Hands Below

Contact Information: info@thewildrosepress.com

Cover Art by *Angela Anderson*

The Wild Rose Press, Inc.
PO Box 708
Adams Basin, NY 14410-0708

Visit us at www.thewilderroses.com

Publishing History
First Scarlet Rose Edition, February 2013
Digital ISBN 978-1-61217-810-3
Print ISBN 978-1-62830-128-1

Published in the United States of America

Dedication

To the heroic Italian Coast Guard captain
whose commanding voice was heard
around the world.

To the United States Navy who took me on my first
Dependents Cruise. The ship left Pearl Harbor,
Hawaii, and sailed its short, merry way
to the neighboring island of Maui
with excited families on board.
It was an experience never to be forgotten.

Chapter One

7 Night Western Caribbean Cruise aboard the Sea Sapphire

Day 1

"Are you sure it's safe down here?"

Liam Rossi ducked his head out from under a ventilation shaft as the sultry query floated up to his ears. Stuffing his flashlight into the pocket of his coveralls, he scrambled down the vertical ladder and onto a catwalk in the steamy engine room of the Sea Sapphire.

"It's safe, lovely Evie," came masculine assurance from down below. "And, perhaps the only place I can have two minutes of peace without interruption."

Liam rubbed at the kink lodged in his neck and frowned down at the face of his watch. Ah, yes. It was that time again—the twilight hour. The *courting* hour. He peered at the couple standing in the corridor below.

The woman raised sun-kissed arms and curled them around her companion's neck. Her long throat arched up from an action-packed body whose Christmas-red gown clung to some pretty dangerous curves. Full-sized breasts tanned to a honeyed sheen pillowed up against her companion's uniform dress whites.

When she tilted her face to gaze up at her partner, Liam stared, arrested by the wide-set eyes, delicate sloping cheekbones, strawberry wine lips,

1

and a pert nose.

Beneath a flare of smoky topaz lashes, blue eyes simmered with a look so full of desire Liam suffered a fierce stab of envy for the other man.

"We could go back to your cabin," she offered, her voice lilting hopefully.

"I'm on duty. I should not even be here with you."

"Then come to my cabin later. When you're off duty."

"Not allowed, unless it's official business. But you're here, I'm here and...I'm on fire for you, Evie. I want what's between those legs, sweetheart. Here."

"Now?"

"Yes, now. We could have our own cruise ship mile-high club." Her companion nuzzled her neck. "Where is your sense of adventure, hmm?"

It's not in her pants, genius.

With a sweep of his finger, the other man coaxed one luscious, quivering breast out from behind its velvet slash.

Hot *damn*! Liam smothered a groan. His taste buds puckered and his mouth watered at the sight.

"Look...at...you. Mm-mm-mmm!" The other man breathed and cupped that golden, buoyant mound in his hand.

Concealed in the shadows, Liam watched him squeeze her breast until its pink peak jutted into a pout. The man fingered the wanton nipple to pudgy elongation till it looked like a plug of cotton candy. Then he guided that tender morsel and its creamy, weighty flesh inside his mouth, deep as it could go, and began sucking.

"Ahh..." The woman's gasp shot a sexual charge down Liam's back, but a frown marred the sweet contour of her lips.

What do you think, sweetheart? Liam mused.

Time to move the party somewhere else?

She sighed, cupped the man's jaw, and slid a finger inside his mouth to break the rigorous seal his lips had on her tit.

"Evie!" The man protested, pawing at her glistening nipple.

She grabbed her partner's hand and gazed, exasperated, into his face. "Slow down there, speedy."

"Why?"

"Because I want to have some fun with you in a *bed*, that's why. The silk sheets I brought on board are the color of Belgian chocolate. They've never been used." She kissed his fingers.

Liam drank in a pensive breath. Heat sparked from the pit of his stomach and lit into his cock with a sharp, hot singe.

While he struggled to hear what she was saying, his gaze remained fixed on her breast, its rosy innocence rubbing against the officer's dress whites as she pleaded her case.

"Come to me when you're ready, Robert. I want to be with you, but—" she winced. Overwhelmed by the roar of marine diesel engines, she yelled louder, "Not here."

Robert? Chief Security Officer Robert Montero?

Oh *hell* no.

Liam swung out from the shadows and landed on the rubber soles of his boots with a *whump* in front of two startled bodies.

"What the—"

"Officer Montero, how is your wife and baby son these days?"

"Umm…well…"

"Wife?" The rosy flush in Christmas Beauty's cheeks deepened to an indignant red. "Robert, you're *fucking* married? With a *baby*?"

3

"Evangeline, I—"

"Your presence is needed on the bridge, officer."

"Of course." The other man tripped over his feet, eager to escape the frosty edge in Liam's gaze and hotfoot his way to freedom. "Evie, we will talk later."

"No. We won't."

The other man hurried from the engine room, leaving Liam to wade through a taut silence with the other man's catch of the day. Or night.

"You're in a restricted area, miss," Liam said, no stranger to the party's-over look that crept into her eyes. Her reality ship had just docked, but that usually happened *after* a cruise. This ship had just set sail.

Two engineers came clattering in. She stiffened at the sound of voices drawing near. When he flicked a pointed glance at her breast hanging out in the open, she looked down at herself in dismay.

"Ohh!" Hastily she restored the hill of flesh behind her gown, but the image of her silky hand tucking her breast behind a swatch of red velvet had already branded his memory cells.

The men strolled by. Liam nodded. They nodded back, then gawked at the woman next to him. As one of them ran into a load-bearing pole, Liam guided her away through a maze of machinery and up a ladder, beyond a door, and out of the engine room.

Once inside the safety of an interior corridor, she sighed. "It seems other things were off limits, too." She looked up at him as she removed moldable earplugs.

Misty blue lilacs, Liam thought. As he summed up the color of her eyes, muscles deep in his body throbbed with a blistering awareness of this lethally sexy woman.

He took the earplugs from her and stuffed them in one of his pockets, noting with relief how the baggy cut of his coveralls toned down the ramrod salute of his cock.

"Thanks for what you did back there," she said to him. "You just saved a married man from being naughty, and me from umm…getting…ah…"

"Fucked?"

"Yes. Right. Thanks for sorting that one out for me."

Liam shrugged. "Do yourself a favor and avoid men in dress whites altogether."

She studied the blue coveralls he wore. "Why?"

"Ship's officers meet beautiful women all the time, so you're out of luck if it's roses and forever you're after. Only on a cruise ship do one-night stands last the entire voyage."

Her mouth quirked up. "Thanks for the warning, but I think I can handle a man in or out of uniform."

Liam's gaze narrowed. "Then pick one who isn't wearing a wedding ring."

Her long dark lashes flickered. "Robert wasn't wearing one."

"Funny things rings," Liam drawled. "They slide off at the most convenient times."

"Really? Are you speaking from experience?"

Excitement rioted under Liam's skin. Even his scalp tingled from the challenge that sparkled in her eyes.

He grazed his fingertips down her arm and drifted closer to her, drawn to the floral notes that misted the air around her.

"Maybe."

A blend of spring roses and something else, something fragrant like red, oaky wine, ripened his tongue with anticipation. She would taste as good as she smelled. No doubt about that.

Liam's fingers closed over her hand. He raised it to his mouth and feathered his lips along her silky-soft knuckles. "After all, it does get lonely at sea."

****

Evangeline Spencer gulped as dribbles of *want* soaked through her panties.

Pleasure raced down her thighs and her fingers trembled against the caress of the sexy mouth belonging to this dark-haired stranger. A man who'd stepped in before she and Robert took things too far.

He'd known Robert was married. Yet he risked the wrath of his superior by reminding the other man of his wife and baby waiting at home. This man's actions showed a depth of character that intrigued her. What it meant beyond the next five minutes, who knew?

Evie, proceed with caution! So he has a sex-god face, and a voice that turns your legs to stacked marshmallows, but a heart under the pretty red bow is priority number one.

His mouth glided along her skin, and when her eyes met his, dark and cool like mountain moss, she didn't mistake the glint of humor that flashed in them.

Taking that as a warning flag, she jerked her hand away. It would be a damn shame if he expected some sort of reward for doing the right thing!

"I see." He straightened and arched a sleek brow. "So, you want an officer and a gentleman, hmm? You know the two aren't always one and the same?"

"I don't see an officer or a gentleman anywhere, so I wouldn't know."

He looked down at his coveralls and shot her a wicked smile. "I guess you haven't heard the latest word on engineers. We'll keep your motor running—all night long."

"Hmm, I missed that news flash in my Portland paper. Well, it's been fun but I have to go enjoy the rest of my cruise. Bye-bye."

She turned to leave, but long fingers closing on her upper arm pre-empted her dash to freedom. The touch of his hand on her skin, the hint of cedar in his aftershave mingling with the scent of leather and diesel fuel, made her hot all over!

Her perky nipples must have poked his chest when he drew her against him, too. But by the time he'd employed his stealth-bomber moves on her, it was too late to run. Curling an arm around her waist, he hooked her chin with one lean finger.

"How about a little souvenir to take with you…" he murmured just before his minty mouth covered hers.

I cannot believe this! Evangeline's thoughts raced, but she did nothing to shrug off the wild tingle of his mouth exploring hers. It felt…*amazing*!

Heated fingers swept over the ridge of her spine, rising naked above her gown's bare-back design. It was meant to invite a touch such as this— a caress so teasing yet so potent, her pussy creamed with the hot thrill of it. Sensation melted her will. His soft, skilled lips dove over hers and melted her down.

Coiling her hair around his fingers, he tilted her head to give him better access to her mouth.

As his fingers massaged her scalp, he cradled her head to keep her mouth still, while he fed her the steady pulse of his tongue.

My word, does he know how to wield that muscle.

Suddenly she wanted that tongue everywhere! She burned to feel it lick her nipples, flick at her clitoris, and slide into her silken heat.

7

Step away from the engineer, Evangeline, was her last thought before she curled into him like a dazed little lamb.

She didn't resist when he grasped one of her hands and glided the tips of her fingers down along the burgeoning ridge of his shaft.

"Hoo," Evangeline exhaled, impressed.

Trouser bulge rising, his cock was shaping up with impressive girth. And length. Quite the humdinger. Oh, yes, indeed!

Shame on me for taking measurements, she scolded herself, then spanned his mighty length with her hand.

Good grief! The man wasn't getting any *shorter*. His brazen words and velvet tongue mimicking the thrusts of a capable cock rubbing inside the grip of her palm let her know he was up for a sexy-hot romp, too.

"Mm-hmm," he murmured and, licking her lower lip, his hands spooned over her ass as he fit her lower body into his like a long-lost puzzle piece.

She plunged her fingers through his rumple of dark hair and imagined his thickness rooted between her thighs. He tugged on the combs that swept her hair up from the sides of her face and dropped them to the floor.

She knew what he'd see; honey-brown hair spilling below her shoulder blades with strands that cooled to golden blonde highlights.

"Take me on, Evie," he invited in a husky voice. "Let me give you what you want."

His breath spiraled in her ear and spilled down her neck. She shivered. "You don't know what I want."

"Officer Montero dry-humping you while sucking on your tit gave me some pretty big clues." The stranger kissed her mouth. Lavished her lips with lusty swirls and tugs of desire meant to chase away any embarrassment she might feel. He lifted his head to assess its rosy response. "Robert's not here, but I am. And, I don't have a wife and kid to make me think twice."

His thumbs brushed her cheeks, and his gaze probed hers with sensual appeal. "Let me be the one to satisfy you. I can even swing the roses."

Evangeline's breath locked on the pull of his words. Not the part where he noticed her being dry-humped while Robert sucked her tit, but every temptation he was offering. Yet, one fine chunk of man candy he might be, there were certain criteria that needed to be met.

"Can you swing the forever part as well? Because I came on this cruise for that, not just some holiday *fucking*. Make no mistake...I want that, too."

His thumbs tensed against her skin. So she didn't pluck the daintiest terms out of the air, but she had no time to dance around the facts. She was on deadline here.

Her heart thumped nervously in her chest. She'd just thrown some heavy words at him, after all. *Forever* and *fucking* were attention grabbers for sure, but had either piqued his interest?

"Questions?" She hoped he had some to ask. She'd tell him the truth—that she'd signed up for this singles' cruise to find a husband. Or at the very least, the start of something beautiful.

Please show me some interest, Mr. Yummy, 'cause then it would be worth it for me to ask your name.

If she scared him off, she'd simply move on and forget about him. Forget the sultry curve of his mouth, his shameless kisses. His bold touch.

A breath hissed past his lips. Decision made, he shook his head, placed a kiss on her forehead, and let her go. No questions asked. "I'm afraid I'll have to pass."

"Thought so." She smiled at him like a good sport. "Will you show me the way out?"

She followed him up a flight of stairs and out through yet another door. He then escorted her to a utility elevator that would take her up to the passenger decks.

"I can help you with one, but not the other," he offered up with an honesty she appreciated, especially given her forward proposal. "But if roses and forever are what you're after…" The elevator doors swished apart. He waved her inside. "Good luck with that."

Evangeline strolled into the lift and turned around with a smile full of regret. As the doors drifted shut, he touched his finger to his forehead in a nice-meeting-you salute and ended her tour of the engine room.

She brushed a finger against the prickles that danced along her lips.

So this was how it felt to be tempted, tousled, then shot down in flames by a hunky engineer. Nearly getting screwed by one man, then five minutes later slotting *him* in the other man's place. What must he think of her?

And he'd watched them the whole time!

She groaned and rubbed her forehead. Outrageous. Thank God the scruffy devil worked below decks. She need never see him during the cruise. The Sea Sapphire was a big ship. The Western Caribbean was even bigger and would offer wide berth between sightings.

She wanted roses and romance on this cruise, and she wasn't going to apologize to him, or anyone else, for it.

Chapter Two

Evangeline stepped out of the elevator and rifled through her pearled clutch in search of her lipstick.

Head down, she didn't see the figure in the passageway until they collided.

"Oh! I'm so sorry." She rushed to help the older woman to her feet. Her lipstick forgotten, she stared into a familiar face whose bright, hazel eyes gazed back at her.

"Well, hello," Evangeline greeted with a smile of recognition. "We rode the cruise line's shuttle from our hotel to the Port of Miami this morning. Maisy, right?"

"You remembered my name. And you're the hot chippie who helped find the owner of that designer bag I found on the bus this afternoon. Evangeline, is it?"

Evangeline nodded. *The owner must be going out of her mind, wondering where she left her bag,* she'd said at the time. After making a few inquiries, they'd reunited the bag with its grateful owner, then walked onto the ship's gangway together.

The second they'd set foot in the reception foyer, a white-gloved waiter had extended a crystal flute, frothing over with pink champagne. A ship's officer stepped forward to offer her a hand—and a whole lot more.

"I think he wants to get in your panties," Maisy had whispered to her at the time. "He can't take his eyes off you!"

Evangeline now regretted acting on that

11

attraction. Regretted her acceptance of his gift of a special *grand cru*, an entire bottle of which he'd sent to her table later that evening—a table filled with buff, single men.

She thought she'd hit the sexy men jackpot, too. A ship's officer waiting in the wings and hunks at her dinner table made her hopes spin with possibilities. Until she found out that the men at her table were members of a gay choir on holiday.

With no incentive to linger over dessert, she'd excused herself from the table to thank the officer for the wine.

"May I take you on a private tour of the ship?" he'd asked.

Evangeline had purred out a *"yes"* and allowed Robert to take her hand in his. As one passageway led to the next, so began a journey of kisses and caresses that led them to the noisiest area on board ship—the engine room.

"I think I'm lost," Maisy said presently. "I'm not sure how to get to my room. Where's the left of the ship? Where's the right?"

Evangeline tried to hide her smile. "Right is starboard, left is port side, but you have to be facing forward, toward the bow."

"You lost me at starboard."

Evangeline skimmed through the woman's cruise booklet for information. "Right this way. I think you and I might almost be neighbors. So, why are you traveling alone, Maisy?"

"This cruise was a Christmas present from my son and his wife."

She frowned. "You're very brave to come by yourself, but wouldn't you have wanted to spend the holidays at home?" she asked, puzzled.

"Oh, *please*," Maisy burst out with an indignant eye roll. "I would have been ten times miserable with them! In any case, I'm sure they're happy to have me out of their hair for a week. I live with them, you see, in a mother-in-law suite. If only I didn't have such a bitch for a daughter-in-law, the holidays might be bearable."

Evangeline laughed. She could see a DIL not finding this waspy-mouthed MIL so adorable, but she liked her.

"I needed a break from her nit-picking and controlling," Maisy admitted. "Merry Christmas to me! Who knows how much fun I could have for a change. You're here alone, too, I see."

Evangeline smiled. "Yes, I am."

"Things go *no bueno* with Mr. Candy-Man in uniform?"

She shook her head. "No. He was definitely unsuitable," she said, without detailing Robert's marital status. "Oh well. The night's still young. Here we are." She slipped Maisy's pass into its slot and unlocked her door.

The older woman paused. "So, no boyfriend. No husband and no kids?"

"That's why I'm cruising alone."

"How old are you?"

Evangeline paused, startled by how the older woman's eyes shaded from hazel to gold and glowed like a holiday ornament. "Twenty-nine."

The woman's eyes got all twinkly. "You'll find yourself another man soon, don't worry. A lovely woman traveling alone over the Christmas holidays looks quite obvious."

"Secret, secret," Evangeline whispered. "I'm hoping that by the end of my cruise, I can cross one thing off my holiday wish list."

"And what's that?"

"To meet hunky husband material who happens to be great in bed."

Maisy's eyes glittered like diamonds in the snow. "What does he look like?"

Evangeline closed her eyes. "Tall, beefcake build, executive-style handsome. No pretty boy for me. Thirties. Early forties…"

"Sexy eyes?"

She sighed. "Yes. Rich greens with golden champagne undertones." She stopped, dismayed. She'd just described the man in the engine room.

Maisy's eyes widened. "With an eight-inch willy? And great in the sack?"

"Wha-at?"

"Honey, I was a young woman once. I had many lovers back in the day, I'll have you know."

"Well, okay," Evangeline said with a laugh. "Wish me a tiny bit of your luck. I just hope finding *one* man who's a great lover—"

"With a big cock."

"—with a big cock isn't asking for a Christmas miracle. I will settle for a good man if I can't have exciting and drop-dead sexy. But…I'm looking for an all-inclusive deal, you know? Roses and forever."

Maisy's eyes darkened with eerie mischief. "I get it. You want to make a man fall in love with you."

"Something like that," Evangeline said, then wondered why *making* a man fall in love with her sounded like…entrapment. She shook her head. She wasn't out to trap anyone.

Booking this cruise put her on course to making another dream come true. If she found a good man, maybe the third item on her list after "Meet Hunky Husband Material" and "Make Him Love Me" would eventually follow—a baby.

"But don't settle for crap," piped the older woman. "Then again, the way they're making them these days, Santa might have to dig deep in his sack."

Evangeline smiled. Now, if her Christmas

wishes listed *no-strings, booty-banging sex with ship's engine guy…* Well, she knew just where to look.

Scruffy man's mint-laced kisses lingered on her tongue. She could still smell him. Desire puddled in her panties at the memory of his breath feathering her skin, the tip of his tongue teasing her lips.

Exciting? *Yes.*

Mr. Right? *Wrong.*

"Don't worry. We'll get you hooked up with Mr. Hot Pants in no time."

Evangeline laughed at the mischief that quirked up the other woman's lips. "We? Do you have a mouse in your pocket, Maisy?

"No. I just have…connections," she airily replied.

"Well, thanks for the vote of confidence. Is there anything else I can help you with?"

"I'd love it if you could you join me tomorrow for the lunch buffet at the International Bistro. That is, if you don't have anything else planned."

Evangeline nibbled on her lower lip. She wanted to dance till the clubs closed. To find an unattached male onboard ship who wanted similar things—romance, hot sex, and more.

Taking a lonely woman under your wing wasn't in the cruise plan, Evie. This cruise was about you. Roses and romance—remember?

The hopeful gleam in the older woman's eyes wrenched at Evangeline's heartstrings. Keeping a cute little lady company for a couple of hours wouldn't get in the way of that, would it?

"No," she said with a smile. "No, I don't have anything planned. I'll be there by noon."

"See you tomorrow, then. Oh, and Evangeline?" Maisy peered at her from her open door. "Thanks for being my friend. Be careful, and don't hop into bed with any strangers tonight. Wait till tomorrow."

Evangeline's cheeks warmed. "Get your outrageous self into your stateroom!" She shooed the other woman inside.

With a shake of her head, Evangeline strolled off on her merry way, just as the upbeat holiday bells of *All I Want For Christmas Is You* began clanging joyfully through the ship's PA system.

High on the excitement of the holidays and a Christmas hope that her wishes for the New Year would come true, she hummed and broke out in a shuffle, slide, and strut. Shaking her ass and snapping her fingers, she danced her way down the corridor in her high heels.

"Well, well, well," drawled a deep voice from the depths of the interior hall. It slid down her back, warm as butterscotch. "We meet again."

Evangeline jerked to a standstill, then spun around.

The engineer's appearance in regular clothes made breathing downright difficult all of a sudden. His physique dazzled in black pleated twill slacks and a short-sleeved cotton shirt with black, cobalt blue, and bottle green geometric patterns that clung to granite-packed shoulders.

Three top buttons were left carelessly undone and the golden skin showing hinted at a smooth-shaven chest.

He stopped in front of her, a true work of man-art. Crisp, intelligent eyes lasered down at her with interest, and her fingers itched to glide through the satin gleam of his hair.

"Nice to see you enjoying yourself. How are you?"

"Since we met thirty minutes ago? Fine," she fluttered out.

His gaze drifted along her body with unhindered appreciation. "Good."

Perspiration sprouted along her forehead.

He tucked his lower lip between his white teeth and studied her from beneath an inky sweep of lashes. "Are you busy?"

Yes, I am. Standing around drooling all over you.

"Are you?" she countered.

He smiled in a sure and lazy way, as if he knew she wanted to give him the most wet and wicked fuck of his life. Pure lady lust creamed her already damp panties.

"Never too busy for you." He glanced at his watch. "Could I talk you into a private bridge tour? I could introduce you to the captain."

A private bridge tour? A "private" tour had landed her in the bowels of the ship's engine room.

A private bridge tour. She couldn't think of anything she wanted more and should be *last* on her to-do list with him. But she couldn't help it. She loved the excitement of being around his charismatic, stud-muffiny self.

"The captain?" she asked, stalling for time before she walked away from him. Again.

"Yes, the captain. The guy who drives this boat. So," those insanely long lashes of his flickered, "how about it?"

"How about *'no.'* I have had enough private tours of the Sea Sapphire, thank you very much."

He laughed, and the smile in his eyes kindled to a deeper glow. "I'll be seeing you very soon then, Evangeline…" He lifted a tantalizing brow.

"Spencer," she said, prompted by his interest in her last name, but not prepared to put stock in it. "And what did you say your name was?" she asked him pertly.

"Liam Rossi, at your service, pretty one."

"Well, Liam Rossi-at-your-service." She stepped closer and whispered in his ear, "You'll be seeing me again. But not if I see you first."

Evangeline gave him wide berth as she strode off in the opposite direction, and smiled when his masculine chuckle trailed after her down the corridor.

****

Wreathed in a swirl of fog left by late night rains, Evangeline couldn't make out the ocean beyond the rail.

A drizzle of rain misted across her shoulders and dampened the now deserted decks. Passengers had taken refuge in the ship's nightclubs or casinos, or turned in for the night. Everyone but her.

She closed her eyes and hummed along with the melody of a guitar being strummed somewhere in the distance, happy to be on this cruise despite its disappointing start.

As for the sexy engineer? Well, he'd opted off her holiday wish list.

No harm done, but after her last run-in with him, she'd needed a distraction. She thought she'd find one at the nearest disco, and she was right. It didn't take long for the single men to notice her at the bar. She flirted, danced, and graciously resisted drink offers, opting to sip her own glass of wine at leisure.

Training a sober eye on the people around her—without a steady flow of alcohol going to her head—allowed her to watch prospective suitors get shit-faced, red-faced, and obnoxious. Not qualities she cared for in potential baby-daddies, so she excused herself and left the club for a breath of air.

Alone with her thoughts, she immersed herself in the mist's sultriness. The dampness of the night felt far more enjoyable than being pawed at by drunken strangers.

A desirable stranger occupied her thoughts. She wondered what that luscious man-cake might be up to… He'd be asleep by now, possibly. But would he be alone?

Alerted to approaching footsteps, she glanced over her shoulder. Two eye-catching males, one of them her tablemate at dinner, strolled past with their arms wrapped around each other. She watched them walk by.

Gay choir—1.

Evangeline—0.

Who knew how long she remained on deck, moping over her pitiful scorecard, until a deep and lazy drawl hummed over her body. There was no mistaking its owner. No sir.

"And just like a dream…here you are."

Evangeline turned as the engineer stepped forward and filled the space next to her, closer than he should be given the open spaces all around her.

The smell of his body had lingered in her head all night long. The come-kiss-me gleam in his eyes, his angular cheekbones and sensually sculpted mouth bathing in the moon's glow made her wonder if she dreamt him up.

She should leave. Yet the thought of being alone with him filled her with such intense sexual energy, running off was the last thing on her mind!

"May I join you?"

"Yes. Of course." Her pulse ratcheted up several beats as she faced him. Shivers twisted down her spine, an effect of the smile curving his lips rather than the steel railing pressed against her naked back.

"There's a rule on this ship," he murmured. "A beautiful woman should never be under the moonlight all by herself." He trailed his fingertips down her arm.

Evangeline gulped in an excited breath. Her nipples peaked under her gown, recognizing a most sensual invitation.

Dismissing the danger she faced between him and the moonlight, she leaned closer to him, to those lips that harbored the scent of after dinner mints. This conversation was nothing like the one they'd parted to earlier, and she was eager to draw on it. "I must be a little rule breaker."

The stroke of his fingertips turned into an appreciative squeeze. "You could make an exception to your rules tonight."

"Maybe. That would depend on the prize."

"Oh, I think you'd like this one." He reached out and cupped her cheek, then leaned in and pressed warm lips to hers.

His lips sampled hers, tasting each curve with heated fervor and, when he pulled her lower lip between his teeth for the softest of bites, his mouth turned her body into a smoking furnace.

A sweet ache coiled beneath her belly button. Robert may have been capable of stirring her needs, but Liam Rossi ignited a wildfire.

His free hand stroked her nipple through the velvet of her gown and, as his fingertip circled the halo of her areola, she sighed, closed her eyes, and simmered in the sexual adrenaline pumping through her blood.

He broke the link of their mouths to nuzzle at her neck.

"Let me savor you, Evie," he coaxed softly. "Let my tongue taste what I'm sure is a honeyed clit, hmm?"

His words... His mouth! How thrilling it felt, nibbling her throat. Her imagination ran loose, knowing how good he'd be at nibbling her *all* over. Why not? They knew where the other stood. And a little sexy something to take the edge off her hunger would do her a world of good.

An orgasm was one of the reasons she'd boarded the Sea Sapphire, after all. Not the most important reason, but she'd yet to set her sights on someone new, and a gorgeous man asking to lick her pussy in the moonlight deserved only one answer.

"Ooh, yes. *Please...*"

The velvet strips covering each breast were tugged aside, flaunting her nipples to the damp night. She wasn't sure who'd been the one to do away with the barriers. Nor did she care.

Not when he gently gripped her heavy breasts, squeezed them, cradled their weight in his elegant hands, and aimed their rosy tops at his mouth.

Not when he pulled each of her nipples into his mouth and licked and kissed them intimately. The exquisite suckle of his mouth on her breasts, the lateness of the hour, and the isolated deck created an erotic cocktail that stirred her senses.

So much polish in his technique, she thought, aroused to see his saliva varnishing the tips of her breasts to a wet, rosy shimmer.

He tilted his gaze up to meet hers. "Should I stop?"

Stop? This night *must* end with this man fucking me! Determined to make it happen, she shook her head.

He straightened and dove for her lips.

Strong hands cupped her ass. Slowly he ground his pelvis against the mound of wetness between her legs. Evangeline's lips parted, and she spread her thighs as the hearty length of his shaft rubbed at and demanded access to the slicked tunnel of her body.

His tongue traced the contours of her mouth, then dipped inside to spread her lips apart.

Dazed, Evangeline twined her arms along the rails as he ravished her mouth with his tongue. Her skin flamed with wild delight as he shifted, then dappled kisses down her body, her stomach, her hips—each caress stroked by his breath.

Sinking to his knees, he pushed her dress up her thighs and glimpsed her red bikini panties, a silk strip covering her mound.

"Very nice." He kissed her rounded flesh. The lips enveloping her bikini-waxed slit had her dragging in a stunned breath from the force of his lusty aggression.

She squirmed, eager for more. With expert ease, he dragged the silk halfway down her thighs and buried his face in her pussy. She whimpered. Her thighs trembled.

"Mmm." His mouth hummed against her clit just before he split her thick, wet lips open with both thumbs and planted his mouth on that pink swollen bud.

Evangeline tucked in her lower lip and bit down, her mind in chaos from the delicious kiss of his lips and tongue playing intimately on her pleasure knot.

"Ahh, yes…suck it! Suck my clit…" She crooned her approval of his tongue sweeping across the landscape of her pussy and, when he tugged one pudgy lip inside his mouth, she whimpered.

After devastating her labia with sucks and nibbles, his tongue crested over and against her clit like a tiny set of waves. She plowed her fingers in his hair.

The sounds falling from her lips turned into breathy little pants when he angled his head between her thighs and muscled his tongue up inside her dewy tunnel.

"You are so *good*," she breathed out in a heady whisper, watching his dark head move with sensuous abandon between her legs.

Alluring sounds hummed from his throat as he feasted on her. The enthusiasm of his tongue swizzling inside and around her walls told her how much he loved her taste. With her dress thrust apart, her breasts tumbled free and were draped in a moonlit glow.

They bounced softly as Liam's head shifted between her thighs, allowing his mouth to mate with her pussy in ways she'd never imagined. Spirals of anticipation held her hostage to the pressure coiling deep in her belly.

When he withdrew his tongue, she nearly fainted. Emptiness throbbed where his tongue had vacated.

"Don't stop, Liam," she panted, but her plea was cut short when he blew a raspberry directly on her clit.

Her mind reeled. Sensitive nerve-fibers fielded the erotic signals being thrown at her. Of being filled with his tongue, then emptied, then having her clit tickled, blown on, buzzed on, before he resumed his tonguing exploration of her aching core.

"Too good. You are just too good," she gasped as she ground her mons against his face.

She felt his smile curve against her thighs. He ravished her clit with another intimate kiss before sliding his tongue back into her cunt. In and out...

His thumbs kept her pussy lips peeled apart and, when one of them flipped at her bud ever so softly, Evangeline fought back a scream. Her head tipped back. A rush of ecstasy demanded her mind and body's surrender to the erotic motion of being tongue-fucked by this irresistible man.

She lost herself in the fingers twirling through her trim. When he channeled his tongue into lapping at her clit like his own personal lollipop, he flung her into an unruly orgasm that tore feral breaths of rapture from her lips.

Her thoughts splintered with the force of her release. She stiffened, and her knees locked to keep herself from collapsing on his tongue.

Pleasure billowed throughout her body where

his mouth was fastened, where his tongue darted and licked around her turgid knot. Where his mouth pulled and glided around her folds as her thighs tensed and quivered against his cheeks.

"Mmm. Heaven!" Evangeline clutched the railing with a white-knuckled grip. She moaned, her thoughts soaking up the pleasure opiates that rendered them useless, useless and happy to give way to her body's instincts.

She rocked her hips to increase her clit's friction against the brushstrokes of Liam's tongue. The pulling suckle of his mouth as he enjoyed her texture and flavors added exquisite dimension to the tremors that dazzled her body and sparkled throughout her limbs.

A bone-deep weakness settled in her legs. Not sure she could stand, she closed her eyes, lost in a haze of pleasure. It had been ages, too long, since she'd felt like this, and she welcomed this furious awakening of her senses.

As his mouth and hands cleaned up every drop of juice from her pussy and wrung every pleasured sound from her throat, she clutched the rails hard while the most luscious sensations she'd ever known stormed through her body.

Chapter Three

Day 2
1222 hours

Grrring! Grrrang! Grrrong!

Evangeline snuggled into her pillow and ignored the noise.

Bang, bang, bang!

She lifted her head, looked around, patted the blankets, and blinked. Where was the glassy blue sea? The moonlight? Her lover?

The patterned ceiling above her bed looked nothing like the moonglow that had steeped her in fantasy. And that racket!

She squinted at the time on her wristwatch—except she hadn't brought a watch with her. This trip had been about discovery and dreams, and a watch had no place in them.

Sunlight pierced through her balcony doors and ushered in morning-after reality.

Moisture coated her thighs. Her pussy throbbed with a longing beat for the muscle that had rubbed so slickly, so expertly, against it. Her tongue, laced with the taste of mint, confirmed her still sleepy wanderings. She'd been orally ravished by a man skilled in lovemaking.

The salute of Liam Rossi's kisses lingered on her lips. He kissed as wonderfully there as he did everywhere else. She sighed. Satisfaction weighted her eyelids, and her cheeks reddened with each explicit memory her mind summoned.

She had not slept that deeply in a long time. It felt good to know a full night's rest for a change, instead of the hours she typically spent tossing and turning.

If his tongue was the cure for the years of sleep deprivation after her husband's death, how was she going to manage without his potent form of sleep aid? The man was…unsettling.

More disturbing, he'd also refused to finish what he'd started.

Evangeline—1.

Sexy engineer—?

He'd made her come, noisily, while she'd taken her precious rules and tossed them over the rails, happy to let them sink to the bottom of the sea.

Knowing he wasn't permitted in her stateroom, she'd begged him to take her back to his. But he'd tugged her panties back up, draped her dress down over her shuddering thighs and, without any kind of warning or reason, he denied her.

"Go back to your stateroom, Evangeline," he'd growled. "Now."

"*What?* Come with me, please. Or-Or take me to your cabin if you can't come to mine. I want more, Liam!*"* she'd pretty much shrieked.

He'd silenced her with a hard kiss, marched her to the nearest elevator, and stuffed her inside.

"Liam?" She didn't know what to think. Had she done something to turn him off? Did she…not taste quite like the honey he'd anticipated? Humiliation burned in her cheeks.

The fierce, lingering kiss he'd given her told her otherwise. The way he'd lapped up her juices… Yet, what man had the strength to pleasure a woman and not want to put his cock where his mouth had been and finish the job?

She sighed. For whatever reason, he'd said "*no.*" Best not to dwell on the whys. It still hurt and confused her, though.

Bastard.

She gulped in a stabilizing breath and, while she had no time to overthink matters, her heart softened a little. He wasn't a bastard. A tease maybe…she smiled whimsically.

Shake it off, Evie!

Today? Today was a different story. She had to put herself *out* there. He'd asked for a taste, taken a generous sample, blew her mind in the process, then just—she gulped—shrugged her off.

Be grateful his cock didn't drop anchor in your pussy. It would have felt unbelievably good, lifted your hopes, made your heart spin, only to have him knock you down anyway.

Thank goodness for small favors, she thought wryly. Oh well. She made a mental note to thank him, if seeing him didn't set her off first.

No time like the present to move forward. *Roses and forever, roses and forever…*

She chanted the words in the shower while listening to the ruckus coming from a nearby stateroom, but the clatter drowned out her ability to distance her mind from last night's events.

And what kind of masochist was she that his rejection made her body crave what he didn't give her—his dick? The soap slipped from her hands. Her mind dizzily recalled how lean and long his cock felt, rubbing against her thighs.

Far from relaxed after her shower, Evangeline couldn't hold her mascara wand still long enough to give her lashes a swipe. The clatter next door made her clumsy, and dwelling on the outcome of her vixenish behavior kept a constant stream of wetness soaking her panties.

"This racket," she stuffed the wand back into its tube and flung it down on the vanity, "is going to do me in!"

She threw on her robe and stalked out to the passageway. It didn't take long to isolate the stateroom generating all the noise. She banged on the door. The grinding stopped. Moments later the door swung open.

Dread spread across her chest when she recognized Mr. Delicious stepping into view.

"Good morning." Hot, handsome Liam Rossi raised his eyebrows. He leaned a muscle-bound shoulder against the doorframe and glanced at the watch on his wrist. "Pardon me. I mean…good afternoon."

Evangeline clutched at the opening of her robe, rolled the fabric in her grip, and realized she hadn't put on her robe.

She'd thrown on a thigh-length, cornflower-blue, see-through *thingy* with wisps of skinny satin ribbons that tied around her waist. Those ribbons merely played let's-pretend-to-cover-the-matching-lace-panty-shorts and push-up bra she wore.

His gaze lowered with interest at the treats peeking back at him.

"Hi Liam." Her gaze zoned in on his mouth. Damn. Why did he have to be so charismatic? Her breath stilled against the shock waves vibrating throughout her thighs, and greeting the nerve endings in her clit with sexy little booms.

"Miss Spencer," he murmured. "What can I do for you?"

As her body wasn't in a thankful or forgiving mood at the moment, she gave him a deadly smile. "Absolutely nothing, Mr. Rossi." She paused for effect, then added, "You're being very noisy in there. People are trying to sleep."

A skeptical brow crawled up his forehead. "At half past noon?"

Her cheeks burned hot. *Crap.* Was it really that late?

"Please accept my apologies. The stateroom attendant thought you'd vacated your room. Most of your fellow passengers went ashore, and my work here was only going to take an hour at most."

Evangeline frowned. "Where are we?"

"Key West. You didn't hear the captain announce it over the PA system this morning?"

"I—er, must have been asleep."

"Did you sleep well?" he asked silkily.

She reached up to flick her hair back over her shoulders, aware of how the movement lifted her breasts and made them bounce. *See them and weep, Liam. You had your chance.*

"Oh yes. Very well, indeed," Evangeline said. "And how about you, Mr. Rossi? Did your hand keep you company last night?"

His mouth flattened against her chilly stare. "Evie, about last night—"

"Oh, please! Just spare me, and we'll call it good." She scrunched the flaps of her robe tighter about her body, feeling a lash of satisfaction in the way her words stamped his cheeks with color. "If you'd just stop hammering and buzz-sawing or whatever it is you're doing, I can go about what is left of my morning."

His look was wry. "Don't you mean afternoon?"

"Yes. That." She turned and stalked back to her stateroom, feeling his molten gaze lock on the swing of her ass.

She reached the doors to her suite without tripping, turned the handle, and groaned. She'd left her card key inside. What to do? What to do? *And Maisy has been waiting for me since noon!* "Dammit."

"I'll get your room steward to let you in."

She looked at him and asked, "Don't *you* have a master key or something?"

"I do, but that would take away the joy of watching you stand out here and wait."

"Will you please just unlock my door?" she sputtered, even as she couldn't help but be drawn to him.

Okay, so his rejection shot her morale to the bottom of the barrel, but he surely had his reasons. Reasons she probably didn't want to know like…er, what if her taste turned him off? That would be devastating.

"Very well."

He took his time, sticking the sea pass that doubled as a room key in its slot upside-down, inside and out, backward, and then forward.

"I don't understand." He cast her mock-confused looks in between scorching appraisals of her legs, body, and face. "Why is this key not working? Ah! Success. Here you go," he said.

He held her door open. She strode into her stateroom with two sets of cheeks raging pink for having been so thoroughly plundered by a pair of masculine green eyes.

****

1315 hours

Liam's phone rang as he stepped out of a cold shower.

He strode into his air-conditioned quarters, his body still soaking wet, to answer the call. Maybe the icy wave of AC hitting his skin could wipe that little husband-hunter out of his head, too, he hoped.

Fail.

His body shivered with excitement just thinking about her, while his brain bucked against his fixation on her. He felt like a grade-school boy crushing on his first love.

Roses and forever. Seriously?

Too bad. Hooked and crooked and a wedding band was the last thing he wanted. If only he could forget her taste. Maybe it would stop him from craving the texture of her skin, the sound of her voice, the taste of her, like honeyed silk.

Fuck yes, he wanted more, just…with boundaries. She was exactly the type who would stick her sexy toes in and muddle up the lines.

Tasting her rain-damp body under a tropical moon wasn't something he'd predicted. But with her, anything was possible.

It made her dangerous, and it was all he could do not to risk everything he'd worked for. He'd ached to bend her over the nearest chair and ram his cock inside her pussy in a grinding rhythm guaranteed to make her forget about needing anyone else for the rest of the cruise!

He picked up the phone and paused to clear his throat, then struggled to remember his own damn name while at it. "This is Liam."

"Captain requests your presence in the chief's lounge," said one of the junior officers, snapping him briefly from his thoughts as he toweled himself dry.

"I'll be right up."

If and when he was ready for marriage and kids, well… He had certain requirements in mind for his wife. For the mother of his children. Christmas Beauty was anything but wife material. A fling? Hell yes. Wife and mother material? *Unnk.*

She didn't wear a watch, and she liked to sleep in. Not crimes by any means, but she also took risks. Like traveling alone without friends or family to keep an eye on her, or to spend time with. No kids tagging along.

Was she a woman of leisure? Did she even have family? Friends? The woman he married would need a supportive network of friends and family. How else would she manage those long months when he'd have to be at sea?

He frowned. His mind churned. *Stop this line of*

thinking, Rossi. She'd be gone in a week, this woman who was nothing more than a beautiful stranger. One who showed no fear of being in low-lit and isolated areas on board ship. One who showed no fear of strangers—Christ on a cracker!

He was no better. He'd lusted after and flirted with her. With disaster. What the hell was *he* thinking?

Either she was naïve—or fearless. He wasn't sure which. One thing he did know—she knew which buttons to push to turn his motor on. All she had to do was look at him with those lustrous blue eyes, give him that rosy-lipped frown, and he'd forget himself. Forget his place. Forget who he was and all he'd worked for.

Everything about her spelled trouble in caps, something Liam did not need on this cruise.

So why was he having such a hard time driving her face and her taste out of his mind? He'd wanted nothing more than to whisk her back to his cabin and sink his cock into her core. To make love to her as long as he wanted and in as many ways possible.

He'd picked a fine time to realize that taking her to bed would let her under his skin, too, as she pleaded with him to take her to his stateroom. He could have, especially with ship's security due for deck sweeps any second. Thank God, he hadn't.

He'd worked too hard for the prize that lay ahead. Well aware this woman could mess with him in a major way had launched warning torpedoes straight to his conscience. He'd already thrown caution overboard by burying his face in her succulence as her thighs writhed against his jaw.

She'd taken what he'd offered—what he'd wanted to give. It was enough.

Her savory sweetness tingled across his tongue. Dear God, it had to be enough.

****

Captain Rudolph waved absently in the direction of a pile of papers. "A purse was liberated from its owner in Key West, Liam. Staff managers have been advised and are asked to keep their eyes and ears open. We've also beefed up security as we're sailing full. Let's see if we can't test the Sea Sapphire's advanced security technology, eh?"

"Ah, yes. The automated security screening system, or ASSS for short." Liam's dry observation elicited a chuckle from the captain.

Liam scanned the reports, aware that the system digitally photographed passengers as they boarded the ship, ate, swam, danced—then migrated those images to a visual database for retrieval.

A name caught his eye. "The owner of the purse is Kerri Lorenzo?"

"I believe so. Here, you can talk to her yourself."

He frowned as the older man got up, flung open an interior access door to the officers lounge, and in walked a face from his past.

"I understand that you and Miss Lorenzo know each other?"

Liam's brows rose. His former fiancée was booked on the cruise? Kerri stepped through the door.

"Surprise, Liam." Her voice was soft, her light brown eyes searching. "I thought a week-long cruise to the Caribbean would be a great time to pop back into your life to say *'hi.'*"

Liam tensed. No way in hell did her idea of a *great time to pop back* into his life fit into any definition of his. Not with the way they'd parted. Although he had to admit, he never thought he'd see her amber-gold hair and light brown eyes again. Not in this lifetime.

Not one to forget his manners, he offered her a cordial smile, and hoped it didn't look like he was having a tooth pulled as the captain watched with glee. "Kerri. This *is* a surprise."

"Go on, Liam," said the captain. "Our business here is done. Enjoy your time off."

"Thank you, sir." Liam glanced at his watch and turned to Kerri. "So, have you eaten? Are you hungry?"

"I had a salad half an hour ago, but I could go for a *cappuccino*. If you have time, that is."

"Of course." He ushered Kerri out of the lounge with a wave of his hand. "Are you traveling alone?"

While Liam guided her down a series of corridors, she explained she was indeed traveling alone.

"I'm taking a much needed break before starting my new job as a news anchor in Philadelphia."

"I see. Congratulations on your new job."

Great. An old flame and a no flame were on board. Say goodbye to smooth sailing, Rossi.

Liam's thoughts were grim as they stepped through the crew doors leading to the ship's Grand Promenade. Live trees lit up with fairy lights and potted lavender geraniums evoked the cobbled promenade of a European village.

There were several options for coffee and people watching, but finding a place to sit was a different matter.

"Psst, Mr. Rossi!" A waiter recognized Liam and waved them over to a newly vacated table at the Veranda Café with a panoramic view of one of three pool decks. After they were seated, the waiter hurried off to fill their order.

"So, after I filed my report about my missing purse, I wrote you a note to congratulate you on your promotion," said Kerri. "Captain Rudolph recognized me from my television broadcasts and insisted we meet in person. I hope you don't mind." She met his gaze across the table.

"Not a problem." Liam shifted in his seat, unhappy with the gleam in her eyes.

He knew what his old flame was up to. She wanted cock. His. It wasn't so long ago that she'd been a satisfactory bed partner, too—a woman he'd hoped to marry. Fortunately, he was armed with a more practical brain and a toughened heart these days.

"You're looking great, Liam. And this," Kerri indicated their surroundings with a wave of her hand, "is magnificent. Your ship finally came in!"

Their waiter reappeared with delicate cups of espresso, each topped with creamy foam swirled in heart-shaped patterns.

"I have arrived, yes." Liam lifted his *cappuccino* to his lips. The five years since their break-up hadn't changed her much. A few lines around her eyes gave her a maturity she'd lacked back then. Otherwise, she looked as attractive as ever.

"How have you been, Kerri? Still married?"

She shook her head. "Not as of six months ago, but our divorce was friendly. Due mostly, I think, to not having children."

"Sorry to hear that. So, how did your purse get stolen?"

"I'd just boarded the ship after buying a few baubles in Key West at a tourist trap on Lower Duval Street. I stopped in at the Triton Lounge for a drink, set my purse down on the empty stool next to me, and next thing I knew…it disappeared!"

"I see. And how are you fixed for cash?"

"I have enough in my cabin's safe. Lucky for me I kept my passport in there, too. But whoever took my purse got forty dollars and made off with my driver's license."

"Hmm. Your Caribbean getaway is off to a rocky start."

"I'll say. I've not given up hope for a more satisfying experience, Liam." Her teasing remark and the invitation in her eyes confirmed his worst suspicions.

Shit.

There went his hopes for a trouble-free cruise. Had Evangeline only wanted this from him, his response would have been a personal guarantee to give her satisfaction, but Kerri wasn't Evangeline.

"You've fared well, I see," Kerri rushed to fill Liam's unresponsive silence. "I can't tell you how sorry I was for what I did. Still am, in fact. You were good to me, Liam. I've never forgotten how good we were good together." She took his hand in hers and stroked his knuckles.

"Then you must not recall the Dear John letter you left behind at our Miami townhome."

"That was mean of me."

He laughed, unaffected now by her blasé attitude toward the havoc she'd caused his mind and heart back then.

"I don't see a ring on your finger," Kerri forged on.

He smiled wryly. "I wasn't wearing a ring when I was committed to you five years ago."

"So there could be someone special now?"

Visions of a blue-eyed, rosy-mouthed temptress asking him if he'd enjoyed jerking off flashed through his mind.

Kerri must have sensed conflict. "Let me rephrase that. Is there anyone who might be upset if you and I were seen having dinner together?"

He shook his head. "No. In fact, I will reserve a place for you at the captain's table tomorrow night. We'll see if anyone protests."

She licked her lips. "Thank you, Liam. You—"

A loud crash interrupted her before she could finish.

Liam looked up in time to see their waiter land on the floor. A pair of toned, shapely legs and very familiar thighs in a sunset-orange miniskirt followed, toppling over the poor man.

A little red purse landed next to Liam's feet. He pushed back his chair, picked the purse up and strode over to render aid. He extended his hand and steeled his abs, ready to put up a fight against the enchantment of a pair of blue eyes. "Hello, Evangeline."

She peered up at him, supporting herself with one elbow. "Hi Liam. Sorry. I didn't see the waiter coming."

He helped her to her feet and stuck her purse in her hand. "You okay?" he asked softly, inhaling a whiff of her tea-rose scent, so subtle yet powerful enough to bring him to his knees.

She nodded and smiled up at him. "Yes, thanks for asking."

Liam turned to assist the flustered waiter as he scrambled to his feet in a clatter of ice cubes. He picked up the clear plastic pitcher on the floor. "Carlito, anything broken?"

"No, no. Thank you, sir," said the other man as he took the pitcher.

As staff arrived to assist with clean up, Liam turned to Evangeline, busy plucking out an ice cube lodged inside the tantalizing cleavage revealed by her skimpy top. "You're not hurt in any way?"

She shook her head, her cheeks pink. "I'm good. Thanks for your help, Liam. You look very handsome today." She blinked in shock at what she just blurted out.

He smiled, liking that befuddled look on her face. Perhaps too much. "Have a nice day, Evangeline," he said curtly, then strode back to his table with that ice cube on his mind.

Liam's salad arrived as he resumed his seat. Glancing over his shoulder, he noted a flustered Evangeline searching for someone. He shook his head. Mr. Right, no doubt, he thought sourly.

"Is that Evangeline Spencer?" Kerri asked, staring after her as the object of his thoughts strode past. "Of Portland?"

"I believe so." Liam frowned. "Do you know her?"

"My ex was the attorney who handled Cameron Spencer's estate. The judge left behind a young widow who, before she married the judge, also happened to be the widow of the judge's youngest son."

Liam choked on an olive.

"Judge Spencer left her the bulk of his estate and, while the judge's will was being contested by his other surviving son, he died of a drug overdose."

Liam's gaze followed Evangeline. She wasn't giving up. Whoever she was looking for, she intended to meet.

"I wouldn't be surprised if she's searching for hubby number three," Kerri mused.

"How did she become a merry widow at her age?" Liam wondered. And twice over? What the hell? She looked young, mid to late twenties.

Those silky-smooth lips owed nothing to injectable enhancements. Dark golden hair tumbled around the oval-shaped face with skin that glowed with natural color, not the mask of liquid make-up that some women favored and gave their skin a fake, covered-up appearance.

She was also naturally blessed in the chest department. Those pendulous beauties were anything but fake. Her left breast curved slightly fuller than the right. Yet, they were perfect individually, and as a pair…

Liam stifled a groan. *Feet. Look at her feet, man. Maybe she's got warts.* He looked. No warts. Her dainty feet were tucked in strappy beach sandals that flaunted her red-chili pepper painted toenails. She had the cutest toes, too. Rounded, plump, and suckable.

"Rumor had it that her second marriage to the father-in-law prevented his surviving son from stealing the family fortune."

"Oh?"

Kerri took a sip from her cup. "The judge was dying of brain cancer, I believe. Of course, *she* winds up with everything. But," Kerri shrugged, "by all accounts, she lives a low-key lifestyle on the modest salary she draws managing the judge's charities. His cronies thought she was after the family fortune. The truth is…she got her money in the worst way possible."

Liam cocked his head, struggling to keep the interest off his face.

"Course, there were the huge insurance settlements when she lost her first husband in a car crash. She's known to be very generous with the judge's charities, too. An odd ducky, that girl."

"Very interesting," Liam remarked. Black widow or merry widow—Evangeline Spencer was creeping under his skin.

"I hope we'll be able to spend some time together, Liam." Kerri smiled at him. "It's good to see you again. I sure would love a chance to make up for the past."

"There's nothing to make up," Liam assured her, aware she would present some entertaining ideas on making up, whether he encouraged it or not.

"We'll see." She glanced at her watch. "I've got an appointment at the spa. Is it too much to hope that you won't be on duty tonight?"

"It is."

"Yes, indeed. Feels just like old times. But that's not a bad thing considering all the good times we had. I look forward to more." Kerri planted a light peck on his lips, and then stood. "See you tomorrow night."

Liam watched her leave and knew he could never feel a fraction for Kerri what he felt for a certain woman he barely knew.

"Let me guess? That's the wife or girlfriend you said you didn't have?"

Liam's gaze slid to the thigh sidling smoothly up to him at eye level. Attached to a honey-tanned torso, the burnt-orange floral mini-skirt was draped low on smooth hips. A matching tank top was cropped off in the vicinity of her little belly button.

He took a sip of his coffee, and his gaze flicked up from said belly button to Evangeline's scowling face in a leisurely roam.

Chapter Four

Evangeline placed a hand on the ridged-back iron chair, fighting the temptation to finger the dark lock of hair that brushed lovingly along Liam's collar. If he said yes, she was going to nail him with a good hard slap.

Something leapt in her tummy when his mesmerizing gaze fastened on hers. He reached up, took her hand, and squeezed it. "No. *No*, Evangeline. Kerri Lorenzo was my former fiancée, but she's nothing more than a friend now. How is the race for the roses coming along for you?" he inquired.

"Oh. It's *coming*." She tugged her hand free, relieved he'd been telling her the truth. He wasn't married. Glad that he'd reminded her of what her true focus should be, she asked, "Would you believe me if I said I had a lunch date with an elderly lady, and not a man?"

"I wouldn't doubt a word you say. If you can't find her, you're welcome to pull up a seat and join me."

She shook her head and stepped back. It would be so easy to go overboard on him. Even now he looked sympathetic toward her, thinking no doubt, she couldn't even manage lunch with a little old lady.

She swallowed back a surge of longing. Why couldn't he be Mr. Right? When she'd seen the pretty blonde kiss him, she'd felt jarred in the cruelest way. He might have been married after all.

She'd wildly concluded that maybe, in his twisted way of being faithful, that's what kept him from giving her his cock.

Now that he'd cleared up her frantic assumptions, the emphasis he used to define the other woman's place in his life impressed her. Not that it changed what had gone on between them, or wasn't going to happen between them.

Knowing this, she smiled faintly. "Thanks, but no thanks," she said, and walked away.

Minutes later, Evangeline stepped into one of two glass elevators that traversed the ship's multi-level designer mall, and froze when Liam followed her inside.

"It's not going away for either of us, is it?" He stabbed his finger on the button to close the doors before anyone else could enter.

She glowered at him. "Pardon me if I don't engage in this conversation, Liam. I—"

When he dragged her up against him and fused his mouth to hers, all thoughts of resistance severed from her mind, razored off by the hot male lips charging across hers.

A few glorious seconds later, remnants of brain function kicked to life. The nerve of him! Did Liam Rossi really think he could just barge in here and snack on an offering he'd rejected not once, but *twice* already?

She wrenched her lips away, stomped on his foot with her sandal, and marched to the other side of the enclosure. "You, sir, are not allowed to touch this…" she waved a hand grandly down her body, "…*ever* again."

He rubbed his lips and gazed at her beneath those devilish lashes. "I realize I've got some ground to make up with you."

Ground to make *up*? "Don't bother, Liam. You burned that bridge the night you left me hanging. Besides, I'm after a lot more than what you can give me."

His gaze slitted. "Technically, *I* was the one left hanging, Evangeline. Now, admit it. You know and I know there are things I can give you. Things that you'd love receiving from no other man but me. Why dismiss me for what I can't give?"

"Gee, how about the most important reason: I'm not a seven-night stand kind of girl!"

The elevator stopped. He jabbed a finger at the button that would take them back down five decks.

"What are you doing? That was my floor—"

"Be careful, Evangeline. I wouldn't want to see you hurt. At least you know where I stand and what you could gain from a relationship with me."

"A cruise hook-up, but how about what I stand to lose?"

"Like?" he prompted, as if unable to fathom why docking his tugboat in her canal would be such a problem.

"Like the chance to meet someone who likes the same things I do *outside* the bedroom?"

"A woman like you will always meet men. I can give you what you need now *if* we agree on boundaries."

"Screw your boundaries! And there was never a doubt that you could give me some things on this cruise. But what about after?"

"Evangeline," he said, his voice flush with exasperation. "Worry about after *later*. What makes you think you'll find Mr. Right on this cruise, anyway?"

"I don't. Not really, but if I don't try, then I won't know."

He shook his head. "I would hate to see you hurt."

"Too late for that, Liam," she told him softly. He flinched. "And since when was wanting a husband considered dangerous?"

"According to sources, two have died on you—

ah, shit. I can't believe I said that. That was out of line. Evangeline—"

"Let me tell you something," she fired at him, angry that even on this cruise she couldn't get away from her past. "I loved my first husband. He was a dream—my first lover. He'd been deployed to Afghanistan and was home on leave when he died in a car accident. He was driving to pick me up from class at the university, and a distracted driver was t-texting—*ohh*!" An upsurge of emotion crippled her mouth.

"I'm sorry—"

"Don't apologize, Liam. And," she swallowed back the hurt that curdled in her throat, "I won't apologize to you for the things I want. For what I *need*."

"Evangeline, I want you to know…I find you very tempting. I find…" he clamped his eyes shut for two seconds, "I can't seem to stay away from you, despite your plans and schemes."

Evangeline gulped, melting inside even as indignation bubbled on. "Hopes and dreams," she sniffed.

"Okay—hopes and dreams." His hand curved around her arm. His eyes searched hers. "Will you do me one favor?"

"No. Maybe."

"There are as many weirdos on a floating city as there are on shore. While the ship is equipped with security measures, you are still a woman traveling alone. I couldn't bear to see you hurt while on your—er, quest."

"Husband hunt, you mean?" she huffed, further offended by the addictive heat of his palm. Dislodging his touch from her skin, she took a breath and pulled herself together. "I'm taking a break from my *quest* to explore the ruins in Tulum tomorrow. I'll try to keep out of trouble while I'm in Mexico."

She didn't like the thoughtful assessment of his gaze. "Stop looking at me like that. I have no regrets about the way I've lived my life. And if what you've learned about me hasn't been to your liking? Well, I'm *not* sorry!"

He lifted an eyebrow. "Do I act like a man avoiding you? Afraid of you?"

That tugged a little smile out of her. If anything, he was now a man in pursuit.

"What I did to you on that deck was wrong." His mouth tightened. "Rather, what I didn't do. I see that now—and frankly? I love that you're woman enough to hold out for what you really want. You may not believe this, but I thought I was doing the right thing at the time, for reasons of my own."

"Well, spare me your reasons. It's not important now."

"Would you like some company tomorrow?"

"No," she lied, but knew it was the best answer.

His smile was tinged with regret. As it should be, she thought, trying to be a hard-ass, even as she longed to take him up on his offer. She didn't trust him, and she trusted herself far less.

"Make sure you wear lots of sunblock. Take care of that beautiful skin of yours."

"Well, there goes my topless tan," she sighed. "Despite what you think, there is more to me than the airhead out to snare a husband."

"I don't think of you as an airhead," he murmured. "And for the record—masturbating after denying myself your pussy? It sucked."

The elevator stopped. Her heart skipped a beat.

She wished the elevator doors wouldn't open. That the ship would lose power and leave them stuck inside. As her mind urged her to run from him and the outrageous things he was saying, the rest of her ached for an excuse to linger in his wicked presence. "Wow. That makes me feel so much better, Liam."

He chuckled. "If you don't find what you're looking for, come see me, hmm?"

"If every man on board dies from a plague, I'll think about it." Was he crazy? She'd see him all right—as a last resort!

Evangeline swallowed back her longing to take him up on his offer. There'd be other cruises. Other opportunities. But what if her Christmas wishes could come true on this cruise? She stood to gain everything she ever wanted—if she could just stay away from him.

The elevator doors slid apart.

"Enjoy your day," he called after her as she slipped away.

****

Evangeline found Maisy back in her stateroom.

"I waited an hour for you, Evangeline. When you didn't show, I returned to my suite to get into my swimsuit, which I seem to have misplaced." Maisy bustled around in search of her swimsuit. "They're offering aqua exercise classes that I don't want to miss."

"I'm sorry I let you down, Maisy. I overslept. Then I went to the Veranda Café instead of the International Bistro."

The older woman studied the shadows under her eyes, curious. "What on earth were you up to last night?"

Evangeline sighed. "You don't want to know. Anyway, let me make it up to you. I made reservations for a mani-pedi and a spa treatment. How about you join me?"

"I'd love to! But I don't have reservations."

"I do. For two."

"For two?" frowned the older woman.

Evangeline blushed. "I made them in advance. Just in case I hooked up with someone."

"By day two? Ha! You think ahead, I like that. It'll be my pleasure to join you."

"Did you know," said Maisy an hour later as they applied warm, richly colored *chakra* mud all over their skin, "of these Mayan ruins—Chichen Itza, Tulum, and Coba, Coba boasts the tallest of the temple pyramids in the Yucatan. It's called the Nohoch Mul and stands twelve stories high. You can climb the steps to the top."

"Ah, but Tulum has what Coba doesn't have— a cute little beach. Besides, I'd rather swim than climb."

Evangeline breathed in the eucalyptus and clove-infused steam filling the exotic bath, tiled in magnificent blue mosaic designs.

While glad for Maisy's company, she'd hoped to connect with someone to share the couples' treatment sooner. They'd be rubbing the mineral-rich mud into each other's bodies right now, she mused, feeling her skin come alive from the mud's detoxifying elements.

While it pleased her to see Maisy enjoy the perks meant for someone Evangeline hadn't met yet, she had to admit...Liam Rossi cornering her in the elevator today had boosted her spirits.

He made her feel alive from *inside.* He helped her see herself in a different light—as a woman who had the ability to twist a man like him up in knots.

"Why didn't you book the Mayan tour, Maisy?"

"Because, my dear, while everyone else is off exploring, I'll have the ship's pool and amenities all to myself."

"Very clever." Evangeline hadn't given the other woman enough credit. Maisy was no scatty-headed sweetheart. She was glad to know she wouldn't have to Maisy-sit on her first shore tour, either.

After all, she could very well meet someone special.

Chapter Five

Day 3

Any thoughts about meeting someone took a back seat to Evangeline's shore tour of the cliff-side ruins in Tulum.

She roamed the immense, sunbaked landscape and explored ancient temples and structures long since dug out from the surrounding jungle. A tour inside some of the larger buildings wasn't an option as much of the area had been roped off.

The former glory of an ancient civilization was far from anything she'd yet to see in Portland, she thought, gazing up at the mysterious carved masks of the Temple of the Frescoes, their ancient faces pointing out from the temple's corners.

While an occasional breeze swept through the ruins, the sun beat down without mercy, getting her hot, sweaty, and eager to jump into the crystalline waters below the limestone cliffs the city was built on.

Only when she felt like a roasting pepper in need of a hosing did she make her way down the staircase that led to a charming beach below *El Castillo.* The Castle, an imposing structure, loomed over land and the very sea that Spanish expeditions sailed upon when reaching the Yucatan peninsula.

On her way to the beach, she noticed a small army of lizards basking in the sun. Sprawled out on sand and stones, a few more lurked in the shade of rocky nooks.

As interesting as the ruins, some looked

monstrous enough to dwarf a small dog, but their *I am the king* posturing didn't stop her from her mission of sinking her feet into the buff-colored sand.

Hoards of people had the same idea about a cooling swim, but Evangeline and her towel managed to find a spot along the shore. Moments later, she was swimming in a turquoise sea so pristine that when she opened her eyes underwater, grains of sand reflected the shimmering sunlight.

After taking a break to reapply sunblock all over her skin, she sprawled out on her towel and dreamed of a fearless corsair, a dark pirate dazzling her pussy with his cock along the shoreline, where the sea wasn't the only thing licking at her body.

"If we want to make it back to the ship in time, we need to get moving."

Evangeline opened her eyes. No cute pirate loomed over her with a cock in hand.

Instead, a present-day male gazed down at her with rugged blue eyes that contrasted nicely with his full crop of spiky brown hair. She placed him in his mid-thirties and liked his smile right away.

He held out a hand to her, and she took it, grateful for the help up.

"I didn't realize what time it was." She shook out her towel, tossing sand everywhere. "Thanks again."

"Um, watch the iguana—"

She scurried into the stranger's arms as a lizard loped across the beach in a flash of green. His arms curled around her in a firm, muscled embrace.

"Sorry about that." She pulled away slowly. "Thanks for waking me up. I would have slept the day away in this beautiful place."

He grinned. "No problem."

Hurrying after the group in front of them, Evangeline felt pleased to find herself the focus of his interested gaze.

Encouraged by his smile, she said, "My name is Evangeline Spencer. You're not on tour with the gay choir, are you?"

His laughter rang out. He took her hand, shook it, then held on to it for several beats. "No, but I'll take that as a compliment. Those guys are pretty damned hot if I may say so myself."

Evangeline's smile broadened. A sense of humor, too, she thought, thrilled to think she might gain more than a tan on the beach at Tulum.

"Eli Buckelew, Evangeline. Very nice to meet you."

They arrived at the ship only to be greeted by a slew of unhappy faces waiting for them on the other side of the gangway.

Liam, dressed in stone-gray pleated pants, a black shirt, and a black leather belt, added a shot of masculine chic to the uniformed crew. The frown he turned on Evangeline deepened. His gaze narrowed to lethal blades when he noticed the male strolling next to her.

"Okay, you rebels," the cruise director scolded. "Cutting it a little close here! Don't let this happen again. We sure would hate to sail without you."

Of course, when it was Evangeline's turn to produce her sea pass to board, she couldn't locate it.

"Could it have fallen out of your bag?" Eli asked.

A minute went by. Two, then three. She rifled frantically through her beach bag. Liam now watched her from behind aviator sunglasses.

She shook her towel out again, praying for her sea pass to miraculously appear. Only after dousing everyone with a fresh sprinkle of sand did Liam snarl, "I'll vouch for Miss Spencer."

"Of course, sir," a crewmember said.

Evangeline gazed at him in wonder. He must have some clout on board ship. "Thank you."

"See Guest Services and get another pass issued immediately," he barked at her before stalking off.

"Well," Eli breathed. "He sure told you."

"He sure did, didn't he?" she murmured. Her skin prickled with tiny starbursts at the masterful way Liam commanded those around him.

"So how do you feel about after-dinner drinks and dancing?"

She blinked and focused on the potential suitor at hand. "I'd love that, Eli."

He smiled. "Ten o'clock at the Wheelhouse Bar?"

"I'll be there." She didn't anticipate the kiss he pressed on her cheek, but felt pleased by the gesture.

"See you tonight."

"See you." Her excited gaze trailed after him as he strode off.

****

Liam watched from Captain Rudolph's table as Evangeline made her way down the stairs leading into the formal dining room, an upbeat bounce in her four-inch heels.

He longed to unwrap the plum velvet strapless gown from the sunny glow of her skin. Then he'd kiss her and demand to know what the hell took the tour so long to get back to the ship. Since the shore excursion was organized by the cruise line, the Sea Sapphire had no choice but to wait on them.

What had she been up to? And the guy who'd been up to it with her, who the hell was he? At least one partially hidden cove existed around the ruins where they could have indulged in some sex-play.

He bounced the possibilities from his thoughts. She'd made it back on board. That's what mattered.

She paused at the foot of the staircase where many male eyes were glued. His heart rapped in his chest as his gaze stroked over her hair, trailing the shimmer of silk that spilled down her shoulders in rich browns and then shading to summery blonde lights.

She'd also accepted the regal blue rose he'd sent her—fresh and in bloom from the ship's flower shop—with a note he'd handwritten that said *I'm sorry.*

Restless, he'd squirmed in his seat in anticipation, waiting to see if she'd wear his rose, and he got his answer. Except...she hadn't picked an ear to place the rose behind, to let him know whether or not she was available. She'd tucked it in her dress—centered it in the buoyant pout between her breasts.

Look on the bright side, Rossi. The florist didn't screw up and send her a red rose. That would mean *love.* The blue rose meant the *impossible* and *unattainable.* Obviously she knew the meaning of the color blue.

Message sent. Reply received, darling, Liam thought with heightened admiration.

"Popular girl, isn't she?" Kerri tapped him on the shoulder.

Her effort to capture his attention couldn't clear his mind of the vixen across the room. He said nothing, but caught a swish of Kerri's perfume—modern, chic, and unlike the spicy tea rose he'd developed a preference for lately.

He battened down the urge to look up again and smiled at Kerri, instead. He should stop being stupid. Kerri was a sexual partner guaranteed to please.

On the other hand, Evangeline Spencer would blow him right out of the water in a heaving orgy of senses he couldn't begin to fathom. And shouldn't.

"Is this seat taken?"

Liam looked up and found himself face-to-gorgeous-face with the object of his desire.

She arched a sleek brow. Her eyes glinted with laughter, enjoying the idiotic expression he surely had plastered on his face.

Liam glanced at the empty seat to the left of him. "That seat is reserved. The guest happens to be late—"

"Ah, Miss Spencer!" Captain Rudolph boomed. A jovial grin lit his face as he stood up to greet her. "Glad you could make it."

Liam rose. So, Christmas Beauty had been invited to dine at the captain's table tonight. He pulled out the empty chair between himself and the captain.

"Sorry I'm late."

"What else is new?" he murmured in her ear.

She moved into the seat he withdrew for her. Her arm brushed against his.

"Sorry," she apologized sweetly.

Liam's cock leaped, a hair-trigger reaction. Quickly he took his seat, but not before he smelled his rose on her. His gaze flicked to its brazen placement between her succulent tits and his mouth flooded with want. Her nipples had felt like knotted silk when he'd rolled each one around on the tip of his tongue.

He caught her staring at him. Or was it that she caught him staring at her *and* her rose?

She smiled like a crafty jungle cat, lowered her lashes, flicked a glance at the rose tucked in her décolletage…and never looked at him again for the rest of the meal.

****

"How does someone so young and pretty have two men die on her like that?" Kerri pondered over drinks in the Wheelhouse Bar.

Liam shrugged. "Perhaps she's…misunderstood."

She studied him, a thoughtful glint in her eyes.

"You're attracted to her. I sensed it at dinner."

"She is an attractive woman," he affirmed, irked at how easily his ex saw through him. Not about to discuss Evangeline with Kerri, he asked, "Would you like to dance? Or do you just want to sit there and talk about another woman all night?"

She laughed and followed his lead when he stood. "Liam, Liam." She floated into his arms. "How ever did I let you get away from me?"

He shrugged, his thoughts in conflict as he swung her onto the dance floor.

A man. She'd returned to the ship with a man. *Well, what'd you think, genius? That a woman like Evie would go unnoticed wandering around a crumbling archeological site?*

"Earth to Liam. You're quiet."

"Just thinking. Am I supposed to talk while I'm dancing?"

Kerri ran her palms warmly along the taut muscles of his back. "That could be dangerous. Don't think. Just do," she said, and kissed him.

He accepted the familiarity of her lips, but didn't get a chance to enjoy it. Someone bumped into him from behind. Liam lifted his head.

"Sorry," apologized the man as he escorted his partner past them.

It was Kerri's turn to stiffen as Evangeline walked by. She caught Liam's eye and stopped.

"Well, hello, Mr. Rossi. Eli and I were just going to grab that table over there," Evangeline said, and made introductions. "You two are more than welcome to join us."

"No, thank you," Kerri declined snippily.

Evangeline smiled at her. "It was nice meeting you this evening, Kerri."

When Kerri didn't reply, Evangeline's gaze met Liam's. A playful gleam shimmied in their depths. Something hip-hopped in his gut, and every muscle in his body vibrated with helpless want.

"Good to see you as well, Mr. Rossi." Evangeline smiled up at him.

"Glad you received an invitation to join us this evening," Liam replied. Longing hooked at something deep in his chest.

"You know," Kerri piped in, "guests are not randomly picked to dine with the captain. You must be very special, Evangeline. Or lucky."

The glow on Evangeline's face waned. A hurt look edged out the happiness that had lit up her eyes just seconds ago. "It's been a while since I felt special, Kerri. Or lucky. Being invited to dine at the captain's table made me feel I was a little bit of both. How nice of you to spoil that for me."

"Kerri, there's no magic formula for being invited to dine with the captain." The words snapped from Liam's lips in an icy stream. "But, if being beautiful and intriguing is a requirement, I'd say Miss Spencer meets the criteria. In spades."

Evangeline's gaze whipped to his face, her eyes wide. Searching.

"Have a wonderful evening, Miss Spencer," he told her softly.

She nodded, her eyes appreciative and warming up once again.

"You too, Mr. Rossi," Evangeline replied, and walked off with her companion.

Liam marched Kerri out of the Wheelhouse Bar and said nothing in the tight silence it took for him to walk her to her cabin door. "That was downright bitchy of you, Kerri."

She sighed. "Sorry, Liam. I guess it's pointless inviting you in?"

"It is. And I hope that's not the reason you came on board."

Kerri's lower lip trembled. "If it was, I should just kiss my hopes goodbye, then."

"Goodnight," he said, and turned to go.

"You want her, and you're going after her, aren't you, Liam?"

Liam stilled. "I hadn't planned to," came his rough admission.

"Liam, you might try to strictly plan your world, but you don't plan attraction. It plans *you*."

Liam shook his head and left her standing alone at her cabin door, staring after him.

Chapter Six

Day 4

"Female passenger. Injured. Neptune's Grotto."

Liam was on the bridge when one of the ship's plain-clothes security personnel radioed in. He moved to the video console and migrated to a close-up of the activity on one of the passenger decks.

Minutes later, he was striding out of the bridge wing and making his way to the grotto. Liam arrived just as a deck steward scooped the woman up in his arms and started tottering in the direction of the ship's infirmary.

"I'll take her to the ship's doctor," Liam said.

"Yes, sir." The deck steward deposited the injured passenger in Liam's arms.

Evangeline looked up at him, her eyes woozy. "I keep telling you guys that I can walk," she said, running her fingers along the taut ridge of his shoulder.

"Evangeline," Liam sighed, his skin goose-bumping beneath her touch. "What have you been up to? You smell like…rum."

"I was on the jogging track. I tripped and fell."

"What were you doing? Chasing after a man?"

"Uh, jogging, Liam."

He frowned and looked over at the large scrape that razed her knee.

"I tripped when I stepped on a pair of sunglasses and then I did a splendid power slide right into someone's drink."

He shook his head. "There goes your entry for

the Cheeky Bum-Bums and Sexy Legs competition tonight."

"You saw my name on the sign-up list?"

"I did."

Liam strode through the infirmary's reception area and into an empty room. Before she could ask if he was spying on her activities—and he was—he plopped her on the examining bench.

"Stay," he ordered, and left her in search of the ship's doctor. He walked back in shortly with the MD in tow.

While she was being examined, Liam left again, only to return with a chilled water bottle.

"What's the diagnosis?" He pressed the bottle into Evangeline's limp hand.

"An ankle sprain," she volunteered. "I also scraped my knee."

"It'll be swollen and sore for a couple of days," said the doctor. "I'm going to put you in a splint for now to keep your ankle stable, and the day after tomorrow you can wear a post-op boot. Let's wash that scrape up and get some anti-bacterial ointment on it. You banged yourself up pretty good when you hit the deck, Miss Spencer."

Liam frowned when he noticed the wet streak down the side of her cheek.

"You're in a lot of pain, aren't you, sweetheart?" he asked. His insides tugged with sympathy.

Her lower lip trembled as she struggled to keep from crying. Her chest shuddered. She nodded.

He took her hand in his and gave it a reassuring squeeze.

"I'll give her something for the pain, Liam," said the ship's doctor. "It'll help her sleep, too."

"Dammit. That means I'll have to make it an early night, too!"

Liam squeezed her hand hard this time and

glowered down at her. "That's right. No alcohol. No partying."

Evangeline peeped up at him, her eyes devilish all of a sudden. "I can have a party in my room. Invite some company."

"I'm sure you will," Liam muttered, and the challenge in her eyes sent darts of jealousy stabbing around his heart.

The idea of Eli, the man she was with in the Wheelhouse Bar, tucking her in for the night was something Liam couldn't stomach at that particular moment. His mouth thinned. Why should he care? Who she bedded shouldn't make a difference to him. She was a single, unattached woman.

"Like my friend, Maisy," she sighed, rebutting his thoughts.

He relented with a smile and stroked her jaw. "Now that's a good idea," he murmured.

The thought of her loving anyone with her gorgeous body left a metallic taste in his mouth. Especially when the person he imagined her legs wrapped around was himself. And he'd be damned if *her* sweet cheeks were going on display!

Cheeky Bum-Bums, indeed.

He planned to have a word with the Activities Director. This might be a singles' cruise but there were rules of decorum, for God's sake.

He brushed her hair back from her forehead. "Do you need anything?"

"Mmm…" She gazed into his eyes and his heart tensed to see the depth of emotion in them. To know she was laying bare the impact he had on her. "A husband."

Liam sighed, fighting the riptide pull she had on him. The doctor's chuckle kept him from caving in to his need to reach out, wrap her up in his arms, and smother her mouth with a big juicy kiss.

"Call the hospitality line," Liam said brusquely.

"They'll see that you get whatever you want." He turned away, then paused to add with a reluctant smile, "Except a husband. We're all out."

****

1600 hours

Liam pushed the decorative panel of golden walnut back into the base of a raised planter filled with privet hedges.

The sound of a chaise being dragged around grabbed his attention. He stood up and peered through a cluster of leaves. Evangeline, her one knee bandaged and wrapped, moved awkwardly around with the help of her crutches.

Her hair had been twisted and pinned atop her head with a bronze clip, exposing her neck and the sleek line of her shoulders. When she bent over to adjust the backrest, Liam's offer to help was cut off by the lump growing in his throat, and another filling out his trousers.

Her body, in turquoise hip-waisted short-shorts with white lace overlay and a matching bandeau top, arrested his gaze. His jaw bunched. Her features, locked in thought, set his heart pounding with excitement.

Everything about her engaged him, filled him with an itch that could only be scratched two ways. With her. In bed.

He couldn't peel his gaze from her body. Her taut waist, the way her hips tapered to full, sexy thighs captured his imagination. Nor could he brush her exquisite taste from his tongue.

She looked up and caught him staring.

His cock pulsed with lust.

"Do you need some help?" he grouched at her.

"N-No," she stammered just as the man Liam dubbed her Moonlight Cowboy joined her. The other man wheeled along a trolley stocked with a

61

silver tea pot and plates of little pastries.

"Tea for two," he announced.

"Ooh, nibbles! Thanks, Eli."

Liam ducked behind the planter and went about finishing the task at hand.

"What happened to you, darlin'?"

"I went jogging."

"Huh?"

"See."

Liam couldn't resist a glance around the hedgerow for a peek, watching as she loosened the brown elastic band of fabric holding her splint in place.

The way she bent and stretched her body to unwind the dressing from her knee looked so graceful, his cock stretched. Hardened. He forced himself to focus on the task at hand.

Hard to do with an erection raging in my pants.

She affected his body and bedazzled his eyes. Her voice and laughter drenched his thoughts and hammered him with a craving to taste her, to lick every inch of skin on her, over and over again.

He ached to breathe her perfume, from her neck to her pussy to her thighs. Even her cute tiny toes would smell good.

"What a mess. Sorry this happened to you, honey," Moonlight Cowboy sympathized. "I did knock on your door earlier."

"I was napping."

"If you'd answered, I'd have joined you."

"So, what do we have here?" She directed their chatting to the food, much to Liam's relief.

"Cinnamon scones, coconut-pineapple muffins, mango sponge-cake torte with whipped cream. I might have to wrestle you for that."

"How about this, instead?"

The male groan that followed indicated her desire for something clearly *not* on the fucking trolley, Liam fumed. Annoyed to be on the audible end of sexy banter that made his muscles tighten, his mind flashed with images of what the luscious widow was getting up, or down to, with *Eli*.

His jaw firmed. He shouldn't care. *Put her out of your mind, man,* he ordered himself.

"Will you rub some of this lotion on my skin?"

Liam gnashed his teeth. He took a hammer and pounded a nail into the wood.

"What's all that racket about?" Eli asked.

"Don't mind the noise," Evangeline dismissed. "It's the maintenance crew making some repairs."

How about this for a repair, sunshine? Liam whacked another nail into the panel with brute force. More than was needed, especially in the solarium. With its retractable glass ceiling, magnificent waterfalls and climbing ivy, it was designed to offer serenity.

Feeling far from tranquil, Liam finished the job, ventured behind the maze of hedges, and exited the solarium in disgust. Mostly with himself, that he couldn't control his savage reaction to Evie hooking up with another man.

It was only a matter of time. Maybe even a matter of minutes. What did he plan to do about it? Nothing. Not a goddamned thing. She didn't belong to him. He didn't belong to her.

Yet, the thought of doing nothing didn't feel like the answer. At least, his cock didn't think so.

The thought of doing nothing made him feel trapped. Trapped, helpless, and irritable. Irritable on a luxury cruise ship—the place he lived and worked. The place he thrived in.

He'd have to jump overboard. Swim his ass to shore because, God help him, if he had to put up with one more minute of watching yet another stranger drool over and paw at Evangeline's goodies? He was going to fucking lose it.

Chapter Seven

The Tropical Midnight Feast
2400 hours

"*Calypso-o-o!* Step, step, left, right, bounce in your step, body *oscillation…*"

"Come on, Eli." Evangeline tugged him over to the dance floor, putting some weight on her gimpy foot as she snapped her fingers and wiggled her hips.

As one of the ship's bands, Crown Jewel, played island music, the energetic lead singer taught the writhing audience some moves. Poor Eli had no groove whatsoever, but what he lacked in rhythm he made up for in heart.

When the music stopped, he drew her into his arms. "Having fun watching me make a dork of myself?"

"Dancing to the music of a live band at midnight, on board a cruise ship in the middle of the sea? Magical!"

His lips brushed her cheek, then grazed the skin just under her ear. She closed her eyes and shivered.

"You like that?" he murmured against her skin. "Because there's more where that came from." Eli distanced himself from her long enough to help her to a table next to the crowded bar.

He pulled out a chair and waved her into it. "What are you drinking?"

"Something cool and sweet."

He returned with two pink and yellow concoctions of pineapple and cranberry juice, shot with coconut rum.

"So tell me, Evangeline," he sat down and took her hand in his, "why *are* you traveling alone, really? There's more to what you told me last night, other than being a twenty-nine-year-old executor for a charitable organization who's always wanted to go on a holiday cruise. What are you looking for?"

She ran her finger around the condensation chilling on her glass. "The usual. Excitement. Fun. A man to father my children."

"Huh?"

Evangeline laughed. "Relax. He has to be willing and up to the task."

"No shit!"

She smiled at him and sipped her drink. "Did I tell you I'm a widow?"

"Yeah, you did."

"*Twice*. Both my husbands died."

"Oh. *That* I did not know."

"Last night I told you I was married at twenty-four, and that my husband died in a car crash two years later. What I didn't tell you is that when my father-in-law became ill, he asked me to marry him to keep his drug-addicted son from taking advantage of the family assets."

Eli frowned. "Was that a love match, too?"

"No. He had a terminal illness. He was also a rich man who needed someone he felt he could trust. We were both still grieving for his son. Quinn was his only child with his second wife. His older boy, on the other hand, had been known to forge checks and steal family heirlooms to pawn for drug money. While Cam loved and provided for him, he needed to make sure his assets wouldn't get squandered."

"And your role was…what?" Eli asked, his dark eyes reserving judgment till he had all the facts.

"I made sure that he died with dignity. I

worked as a certified nursing assistant while going to school for my business degree, so I was qualified to take care of him. Before he died, he appointed me to ensure that his wishes for his charities would always be carried through." She paused, thoughtful. "Being twice married and twice widowed has flawed me, Eli. But I won't sugarcoat who I am, either."

"It's being twice *widowed* that would make a prospective husband just a tad worried," Eli admitted.

She replayed Liam's elevator comment in her mind and felt a lash of pain over it. "I realize that two dead husbands will hurt my chances of finding husband number three, but I know he's out there. I also believe in third time lucky. The man who takes a chance on me will live a happy life. Loved by me and the children we have together."

Eli said nothing for several minutes. They both sat in thought-filled silence, sipping their drinks. When he finally spoke, he said, "So, other than being able-bodied and willing, what else would you require in your baby-daddy?"

"Friendship, kindness, respect. Mattress compatibility."

His eyebrows rose. The corners of his mouth tipped up in amusement. "You're willing to take him out for a test drive? Let's go, darlin'!"

"Not so fast, cowboy." Her smile teased him. "There'd have to be some romance and chemistry there. Boom, bang, pow, you know? Maybe shooting stars."

"Got it. You want some romance behind your compatibility test-poke," he pondered with a chuckle.

Evangeline took a pull of her drink and enjoyed the tangy bite of the cranberry and pineapple juices. That he was still listening and hadn't yet run off in disgust boded well for him. If not as a potential baby-daddy, then as a nice guy with a sense of humor.

"What's wrong with me wanting to make sure it's good for you? I mean—him? I mean—well, you know what I mean. What he wants is important, too."

"There's nothing wrong with wanting sexual compatibility. It's just weird to see a woman put all her cards on the table like you do, Evie. Did you ever think you might find that person by going about your everyday life? By doing things you love to do?"

"Yes, but so far?" She shrugged. "*Nada*. I needed to shake things up."

"So you sailed away from a safe harbor. Well, you picked a good time to do it. Married men with families don't go on Christmas cruises alone."

A smile spread across her face. "Yup. And I know it's a long shot, but my wish for this Christmas is to have one of my dreams come true. If not, what have I lost?"

"And what if your search could be over tonight?"

Evangeline swallowed back the hope that leaped inside her chest. "What do you mean?"

"I'd like to be that man, Evangeline. To be honest, I came on this cruise to relax and not try so hard to find The One. I'm thirty-nine, and burnt out on the dating scene. Did I mention that I'm here to throw a party with a bunch of divorced guys who married for love years ago, but are now cruising solo? I find you on the beach when all I'm looking for is a tan, and we just…click. This isn't love, but I think it's a good place to start."

"And what is it that you do?"

"I'm a custom home builder." He gave her his company's website address and produced a business card. "Now, don't take this the wrong way," he hesitated, "but any woman I marry would have to sign a pre-nup."

"Of course." She nodded, and thought it best not to tell him her net worth until things progressed a bit. "What are you and your friends celebrating?"

"Tomorrow I'm throwing a bachelor party for a friend. Wife number two for him, by the way. Since I'm his best man, I'm in charge. But I can free up some time for us in the morning. We arrive in Ocho Rios, Jamaica, tomorrow. What are your plans?"

"I'm a bit overwhelmed with my bum ankle. Since my river-tubing Jamaican safari is postponed, I promised Maisy I'd accompany her to the art preview and auction in the morning."

"Who's Maisy?"

"She's this cute, potty-mouthed lady that's adopted me for the duration of the cruise. Or maybe I'm the one who adopted her." She grinned and sipped her cocktail.

"All right, then. I'll be thinking of you while I'm busy drinking and carousing," he teased, and took her hand. "We'll be in Grand Cayman the day after tomorrow, on Christmas Eve. We can tender in to George Town, spend the day shopping and looking at rings so that, if this works out, I have an idea what strikes your fancy." He winked. "*If* your leg is up to it. Then later on we'll talk about getting down to this baby making business." He twirled an imaginary mustache for effect.

Evangeline laughed and liked what she was hearing more and more. She took the absence of warning bells as a good sign, too.

"Sounds like a plan."

Eli leaned over and sealed the deal with a kiss. He drew back and gazed at her lips, amused. "Surely we can do better than that."

Eli's mouth didn't taste minty. He tasted like

cranberry juice. She liked cranberry juice. Eli tongued her. Their lips mashed. She made a few *"mm-mmm"* sounds and hoped for stars to flash before her eyes.

Nice. No shooting stars, but she felt a responsive tweak in her midriff. His mouth moved over hers with skill, and his tongue let her know he was schooled in laying down kisses.

As far as kisses went, Eli's kiss felt pleasant. Comfortable. She and Eli weren't drunk, so no heavy dose of alcohol was at play to warp her common sense.

Although a bit of awkwardness had tensed her stomach up when their mouths first met, it was expected. This was an audition of sorts, after all. While this kiss might not have blown her socks off, it didn't rule out other items on her baby-daddy checklist.

"Mmm." Eli shifted away and grinned, obviously aroused by their brief play.

Her small burst of laughter eased any tension that might have lingered between them after that kiss. "I see some promise, Eli. I see some real promise."

Chapter Eight

Day 5

"Another purse has turned up missing, sir. Witnesses remember seeing this lady in the vicinity."

Going over surveillance video with Captain Rudolph and the Chief Security Officer, Liam studied a cluster of images frozen on the monitor. His gaze narrowed at the blurred face of Evangeline in the background on one of the photos.

He excused himself and strode off in search of her, confident her ankle would have kept her confined to the ship while docked in Jamaica.

He found her reclining on a chaise in Neptune's Grotto. "Got a minute?"

Freshly nibbled green-gold pineapple rinds lay on a plate perched across her thighs. Sunglasses shielded her eyes. She pushed them down her nose. Blue eyes peered at him above tortoise-shell rims, inlaid with the twinkle of rhinestones. "Sure."

Liam pulled up a chair and sat. He clasped his hands together and gazed at a face scrubbed clean and free of make-up. When they'd dined at the captain's table on formal night, he'd not been able to take his eyes off her. Now, in broad daylight, Evangeline's beauty captivated.

His gaze skimmed down her swan-like neck and ground to a halt at his blue rose, fully bloomed, and tucked between her breasts. Before his very eyes, her nipples peaked and pushed against two wisps of fabric.

"And you got those gorgeous nipples behind those silly excuses for triangles *how*?" he growled at her.

She smiled and picked up her drink.

The thought of snatching her drink from her and dumping its icy contents down his pants flared through his brain. His breath steamed up inside his lungs.

As his cheeks darkened with envy at the rose's placement, a tingling spread across his back, rode up along his ears, and dove down into his balls.

"Enjoying yourself?" he gurgled.

Her lips pouted over the straw speared in her drink. "Mmmhmm."

He wished she'd take those damned sunglasses off so he could see the laughter in her eyes and not just feel it ransack through him. Mocking him. Mocking the bulge that threatened the clean line of his pants.

That mouth of hers summoned memories of what it felt like to kiss her. He longed to bury his nose between her breasts, to smell his rose on her and, most desperately, to smell the blossom between her legs.

He cleared the knot lodged in his throat. "There's been a rash of stolen purses as far back as Miami. I need you to be careful."

"Oh?"

"Keep your cash and valuables locked up in your room's safe, and no wandering off to dark corners with strange men."

"Buzz killer."

"How's your leg?"

"It feels a little better. Just a bit tricky, you know? If I bend my knee, I reopen the scrape that's healing. Makes it hard to get in and out of the shower at night and not get it wet, too."

"Hmm." She wouldn't be telling him this if her

71

Moonlight Cowboy was helping her in and out of the shower, now would she?

With three nights left of the cruise, his curiosity got the better of him. "And, are you having much luck in other areas?"

Evangeline stared at the hunk of a guy being nosy about her business.

Earlier, she'd longed for a cooling dip in the pool, but that was off limits because of her knee. Now, here sat Liam, looking like a tall glass of fresh and sexy, and he was off limits, too. Off limits but snacking on her body in her micro-bikini with greedy eyes, while inquiring if she'd made her dreams happen yet.

More worrisome were her thrusting nipples. With his hungry gaze stuck to the rose she'd babied for two days in her stateroom, no way could he miss those ill-behaved discs popping him a dual salute.

Aarghh! This stunning man and his well-versed tongue might've been up close and personal between her legs once, but that didn't make him entitled to know her business. "Have I given up my search, you mean?"

"I wouldn't put it like that exactly, Evie. People have come aboard cruise ships and found what you're looking for…organically."

Ooh, he was annoying. "Hmm, as opposed to my calculating methods? Well, here's the dealio, Liam. I don't have time to play *organic*. My baby-mama clock's a-ticking."

Liam's irises flared. "Ahh. I see a little more of your urgency."

"I'm glad. You sure are above decks a lot."

He shrugged, his gaze intent on her lips. "Yes, it seems I keep forgetting my place."

"I don't mean it like that. I've got nothing against your profession," she assured him.

"That's good to know," he said, but looked a

bit skeptical. "And where is your friend? Ah, Maisy… *Clauss*, is it?"

"*That* was the name on her sea pass, yup. Comes in handy, I'm sure, especially at Christmas. Maisy's gone off with a gentleman friend for ballroom dancing classes."

Liam smiled. "It's very kind of you to keep her company, but… How much do you know about her?"

She laughed and wondered if he was worried for her or for Maisy. "Not much, other than she's got a mouth like a sailor and seems to like me. Maisy is a cutie, and…I suspect she's lonely, too. Who would send their elderly parent on a cruise without company, Liam? At Christmas, too."

"You'd be surprised. There are people who offload loved ones on cruises who really should be supervised. When we notice these individuals, we do our best to keep them happy, safe, and entertained."

Evangeline sighed and hoped that Marshall Capshaw, Maisy's new friend, would save the day. The widower, a retired restaurateur, had been spending a lot of time with Maisy, and they seemed to enjoy being with each other.

Liam glanced at his watch. "We arrive at Grand Cayman tomorrow. There's no docking berth, so prepare to be tendered ashore. I'll make sure that you and your friend get all the assistance you might need."

"I'm not going ashore with Maisy." Evangeline licked her lips. "Eli Buckelew and I—oh, never mind. Eli and I will bring her along with us tomorrow if she doesn't have other plans. That way she's not alone on Christmas Eve."

"Doing anything special?"

"Sightseeing. And some shopping." *And why,* fretted Evangeline, *am I dancing around the truth with this man?*

"Looking for anything in particular? I can make some recommendations."

She gave him a thoughtful look. Since it wouldn't matter to Liam either way, why not share her good news? It wasn't as if he'd care. He'd even wished her luck on her husband hunt.

"As a matter of fact, Eli and I plan to look at engagement rings. He's *considering* marrying me. And, if things go smoothly, I'll *consider* accepting."

His eyes flared, then narrowed. "Well, well. So, there's a possibility you found your roses and forever. Congratulations."

She didn't understand why her stomach tensed, or how he could make her good news seem...empty. Shallow, even.

Neither of them had set expectations for the other. The terms they'd laid out had been shrugged off by both sides, so why did so much furious color belt the slope of his cheekbones?

Her heart squirmed in her chest. "It's not a done deal yet."

Why did her voice sound so small? So...guilty? *Because my heart and my body wants you, Liam. You know it, and you don't care.*

Admitting the truth to herself, she couldn't hold the uncompromising look he gave her. He made her feel impaled. Caught. A fish squirming at the end of a spear. She looked down at her pineapple rinds, worried he might see what was in her eyes...and in her heart.

When he finally spoke, his voice remained level, casual, and cool. "Don't be late coming back this time, hmm? The ship's captain waits for no man. Or woman."

Chapter Nine

Day 6
0915 hours, Christmas Eve

Evangeline glanced at the clock on the wall with anxious eyes. Eli was twenty minutes late.

If he didn't show up soon, they weren't going to make their tender into George Town.

She was still tapping her foot fifteen minutes later, still no Eli in sight. Not wanting to miss their tender, she hurried to his cabin.

Had he changed his mind about going ashore? About *everything*? After all, the glow of a midnight moon and the heady buzz from a cocktail made people say and do things they regretted in the morning.

"Eli?" She knocked on his door.

Her stomach twisted at the lack of response and the absence of noise behind the door. Somewhere down the passageway, a door opened. A woman laughed. A man swore.

"Don't forget your shoes, Eli," the female voice teased.

Evangeline turned. How surreal it felt to watch the man who'd just offered to consider marrying her, backing his way out of someone else's cabin with a woman's arms draped around his neck.

Not just any woman, either. Evangeline recognized Liam's ex.

"I have to go, Kerri," Eli was saying. "It's been nice, but—"

"More than nice. And you don't have to go, do

you? I mean, you could stay," the other woman appealed. "You know you want to."

Evangeline groped at the wall for support. Her thoughts spun as her dreams and hopes spiraled out of reach. She swallowed past the lump in her throat, took a breath, and stepped forward on the wrong foot. Pain shot up her leg, but it didn't hurt enough to stop her.

"Eli." Her voice filled the passageway.

Eli turned. The sleepy pleasure on his face shifted to a round-eyed look of alarm. "Evangeline! Oh, shit."

"It's okay. Please stay. I'll be going in to Grand Cayman with someone else."

While Eli untangled himself from the other woman's embrace, Evangeline turned and limped away. But her bad dream was far from over. She turned a corner and found her escape blocked by a broad-shouldered body standing in her way.

No point in looking up to identify him, either. Only one man smelled like that. Like big country cedar and leather, with smoky notes of sex appeal and…

"Evangeline."

The way Liam said her name made her cringe. He'd seen. He'd heard. And while he and Kerri were finished, she and Eli had barely begun.

"Excuse me, Liam. I'm late for my tender." She hurried around him, limping down flights of stairs instead of taking the elevator to avoid being in any closed-in space with him.

Liam followed her. "Let's go someplace we can talk. I know the perfect spot."

"No thanks. The last thing I want to do right now is talk—"

"Evangeline, hoy! Thank goodness. I haven't made us miss the tender, have I?"

Evangeline grabbed Maisy's hand. "No. You're

just in time. Let's go."

"Where is your young man? I thought we were all going into George Town together?"

"Not today," Evangeline said briskly. "Liam, meet Maisy. Maisy—Liam. Good seeing you. We have to go now." She ushered Maisy ahead, and didn't waste any time scuttling past him.

"I think that Liam fella wants to get into your panties."

"Maisy, please. Not now."

"He's still staring after us. After *you*."

"Maisy, *stop*."

The older woman kept her chatter in check as they made their way below decks to the tender platform.

"Christopher Columbus named the Cayman Islands *Las Tortugas*." Maisy changed the subject as the covered water taxi pulled away from the ship. "Named after all the turtles he saw swimming around the islands when he was blown off course during one of his voyages to the New World. You might find yourself a pirate of your own here, my dear."

Somberly, Evangeline thought of a certain green-eyed male with a rogue's smile. There'd been pity in Liam's eyes today. Why, why, *why* did he have to see her humiliation?

The excited comments from passengers on board the tender as they reacted to the seaside charm of George Town dragged her from her anxiety long enough to offload safely at the wharf.

As she and Maisy strolled across the harbor drive, ocean breezes buoyed the scent of island blooms and market spices used in local cafés and restaurants.

Recent rains had coated the area with a moist sheen, revealing the tropical colors of George Town, from fire-engine red rooftops to electric blue storefronts with pink wooden beams. Nothing could be more removed from the orchestrated, jewel colors on board the Sea Sapphire.

Then again, the luxury ship was about escaping to exotic seas, surrounded by the spirit of hospitality and romance. Sipping champagne while flanked by the glow of honey-spiced woods, ebony laced marble, and hot men had catered to her hopes. Hopes that maybe the Sea Sapphire was her ship of dreams.

How foolish of me, she thought glumly, and popped a painkiller in her mouth.

After a couple of hours of browsing and shopping, Maisy pointed to another storefront decked out with specialty coffees, Scotch bonnet pepper sauces, Caymanian birdhouses, honey, and jerk seasonings.

"We can't leave Grand Cayman without some of their famous rum cakes, Evie."

Evangeline stopped to take another dose of her pain meds. After sipping from the pint-sized water bottle she kept in her sling-back purse, she screwed the cap on and dropped it back inside. Then she limped after Maisy.

"Go have a look around, then," Evangeline encouraged, her ankle throbbing as she waited for the painkiller to take effect. "I'll wait here."

"All right. Watch my things." Maisy placed her purchases, a piggy bank frog and a couple of T-shirts, next to Evangeline, who'd found the perfect spot to relax on a storefront bench.

Forty minutes later, Maisy was still a no-show. The smell of fresh island fish grilling in a pepper-lime marinade at the café next door reminded her she hadn't eaten all day.

After a meal of *wahoo* fish tacos, washed down with sweet, icy cold lime and mint juice, she headed back to the sidewalk bench to wait.

Half an hour later, a stressed-out Evangeline took to the streets, searching for Maisy. Exhausted, she finally collapsed against a shop wall, feeling like a stork with her ankle raised and hurting in its post-op boot.

Sweat glided from her brows. Her arms ached from carrying so many bags. She'd since stuck Maisy's frog in one of them, and if it broke, oh freaking well!

She had no clue what time it was. No doubt, she should have been back at the tender terminal by now. The last tender back to the ship was at two-thirty, and the sun was far off-center in the Caribbean sky.

Evangeline hailed a cab back to the wharf and arrived just in time to see the Sea Sapphire chugging off in the distance, on its way to its next port of call—without her!

"Dammit!"

"Hello. Are you Miss Spencer?" asked an exotically beautiful female port staff member.

"Yes, yes I am! And that's my ship sailing off without me. Please tell me what I need to do to get back on board?" she begged, dreading the worst-case scenario. She'd have to catch a flight to the next port of call and board the Sea Sapphire there, at her expense.

"Miss! Miss! Not to worry. Don't cry! Your ship made contact with the port. There is a tug boat whose crew is willing to shuttle you out to meet the ship. Right over there, miss."

A rusty tug boat bobbed next to the pier. Since beggars couldn't be choosers, she took the life vest handed to her, climbed aboard and, as the craft charged after the Sea Sapphire, she remembered Liam's warning: *Don't be late. The ship's captain waits for no man. Or woman.*

They cruised abreast of the ship to where a

sturdy ladder made of rope and wide slats of wood had been flung down the side.

"Ohh…shoot me now, someone, please!" Evangeline shrieked, her eyes hazy with the swell of tears.

She was expected to climb that thing?

Several hundred pairs of eyes peered down at her from the decks. A few passengers waved and gave her a thumbs up.

There's your answer.

She hooked the shopping bags over her forearms, so livid she didn't care that ocean winds were arranging storm clouds overhead and whipping her skirt around her legs.

Left with no other choice, she reached out, gripped a rung, and began to climb.

"You're doing great!" someone yelled, just as a breeze blew her skirt up, exposing her black thong, ass, and thighs to passengers and crew alike. The pilot of the boat below had given up all pretense that he wasn't looking up her skirt.

Helped on board to a clapping audience, Evangeline did her best to put on a good-natured front.

If climbing up the ladder had hurt her ankle and her pride a little, going home sans man was bound to hurt a hell of a lot more.

Chapter Ten

Liam sank his teeth into his knuckles as he watched Evangeline climb up the ladder.

You can do this, baby. Just…don't fucking look down.

He didn't find out that she had missed the last tender until the Sea Sapphire was underway. He'd just assumed she'd made it back in time, especially after his warning.

Only when the ship was sailing from Grand Cayman did Maisy inform him, with much fretful hand wringing, that Evangeline had simply taken off to parts unknown. Oh, and did he know if she made it back in time before they sailed?

What the hell?

Liam hauled ass to the bridge and barely managed to convince the stubborn captain to reduce their speed and allow the tug to meet up with them. He reminded him of the injuries she'd sustained on board ship that might have kept her from making the last tender.

"The ship should have made accommodations to wait for her safe return, sir," he'd pleaded his case.

The old navigator finally relented and ordered the engines powered down to reduce their speed.

"Evangeline," Liam breathed her name. His heart thudded sickly in his chest. After all she'd been through…

He'd sought her out that morning to talk her out of her madcap *bachelorette* scheme, and to tell her the truth about his position on board ship.

When housekeeping pointed him in the direction she was seen heading after having Buckelew paged, he didn't expect to see the man backing out of Kerri's cabin with Evangeline looking on!

Comforting her had been his priority, but she'd rejected him outright. The chance to tell her the truth about his role on board the Sea Sapphire had also been lost.

She was about to find out who he really was and—after she'd puffed her way up the embarkation ladder—it wasn't going to be pretty.

****

"Evangeline, you made it! Thank heavens you're okay."

Evangeline glared at Maisy. The woman was going to be the death of her, along with her broken almost-engagement, her non-fiancé's betrayal, and the hunky ship's engineer. Or maintenance guy. Or whatever the hell it was that Liam Rossi did around here!

"I'm not okay, Maisy." Evangeline jerked angrily out of the life jacket. "Why did you leave? I spent hours looking for you!"

Maisy's forehead puckered in confusion. "I ran into Marshall at the rum cake outlet. We back-tracked to go looking for you, but you'd wandered off."

"You were taking forever, and I was hungry. You could have waited when you saw I was gone!" She extended Maisy's purse to her. "Take it. And take this, too." She plunked the bag with the frog and T-shirts into her arms. "It was all I could do not to drop them in the water while I humped my way up the ladder."

Maisy took everything, then shoved the purse back at Evangeline. She glanced around nervously. "That's not my purse."

"Of course it's yours."

"I've never seen it before."

Suddenly Liam and Kerri were stepping into their heated huddle. Liam grabbed Evangeline's hand. His gaze burned anxiously into hers.

"Are you all right?" Hawkish brows arrowed down in concern, while the other woman peered closely at the purse she was holding out.

"Liam!" His name burst from Evangeline's lips in shaken relief. She swallowed and looked around. Her brows knitted in confusion. Navy blue and pearl gray balloons bobbed festively in the air. Elegant canapés were arranged on decorated tables.

Ship's staff and department officers in white dress uniforms looked on with interest, including Robert Montero who stepped forward to join them.

Flustered, her gaze settled on Liam. In formal dress whites, he exuded sophistication. While he radiated authority, his chiseled male beauty owed nothing to the crisp outline of his officer's...*uniform*?

"What have I missed *now*?" Befuddled, she stared hard at the immaculate lines of his dress whites. "A costume party?"

"Recognition of a new command ceremony." Liam squeezed her hand. "Mine."

Evangeline frowned and studied those smart gold bars on his shoulders. She counted those bad boys again, just to be sure. One, two, three, four...they were all there.

She jerked her hand out from his and raised shocked eyes. "You're a-a—"

He nodded.

"Liam, how does she not know you're a *captain*?"

Pain throbbed in her ankle. Liam in uniform and his mind-jumbling closeness played havoc with her thoughts. The last thing she needed was Liam's ex *and* Eli's other woman butting in at the moment.

"What business is any of this yours?" Evangeline snapped.

"I'm the owner of the purse in your hand—that's my business!" the other woman sniped back.

Evangeline reached inside the purse, grabbed the leather embossed wallet, and flipped it open. She swept the wallet up to her eyes and stared in disbelief. Sure enough, the face of Kerri A. Lorenzo of Los Angeles, California, smiled back at her.

She sighed and handed the purse over to its rightful owner. Maisy had conveniently disappeared, of course.

"Shall we have her detained, Captain Rossi?" Robert Montero questioned.

Liam's gaze took on a brittle gleam as he stared the other man down. "As the Sea Sapphire's Chief Security Officer, you'll assign yourself officer of that watch, no doubt. Please escort Miss Spencer to the infirmary. She may need medical attention."

"I don't want to go to the infirmary." Evangeline's insides rebelled. He'd ignored her for most of the cruise. Now, when her dreams had bottomed out, he was all over the place *and* in charge?

"I see." Liam stroked the angular line of his jaw. "If you prefer, I can have Officer Montero escort you to your stateroom, instead. Your cruise companions have been anxious for your safe return."

"Really?" She looked around. Maisy had ditched her. Eli was nowhere in sight. Her ankle hurt like a little devil. Suddenly, it hit her at the worst possible time, in front of hundreds of strangers—she was a failure.

The tint of pity in Liam's eyes wrung a defeated noise from her throat—a cross between a whimper and a hiccup.

He knew she was a failure, too.

She'd failed in all she came on board to find. Being escorted back to her cabin like a petty thief would so *not* make her day!

She sniffled. Her gaze strayed past the rails. A running jump overboard into the sea sounded good right about now. Except she'd probably trip, fall, crack her head open, and break her other leg en route.

Evangeline regarded Liam with a plea in her eyes and whispered, "I don't want to go to my cabin. My ankle left me confined to the ship in Ocho Rios and kept me from activities I'd signed up for."

A muscle in Liam's jaw ticked in deadly beats. Had they been alone, she was sure he'd have gotten her to comply with anything he asked. But a deck full of gawking passengers gave Evangeline the boost of courage needed to defy him.

They'd cheered her up the ladder from hell. Pictures of her ass were surely going viral on social networks, so what else did she have to lose?

The steely glint in his eyes warned her of danger up ahead. Suddenly, she knew how a baby penguin might feel, looking for its mamma as a hungry shark watched close by.

"So tell me, Miss Spencer, what would give you *complete* satisfaction at the moment?"

Evangeline swore a feral flash of his tongue licked the corner of his mouth. Her mons practically purred in response.

"I'm ready to have that talk you wanted earlier, but I'd prefer to do that in your cabin, Liam. Where we won't be interrupted."

Gasps and giggles circled them. Several males hooted with approval. Liam's jaw clenched in protest, but Evangeline stood her ground. Her stubborn gaze taunted him: *What's it going to be, captain?*

****

Liam's quarters were made up of three spacious rooms designed for comfort and efficiency.

Evangeline's feet sank into thick and cottony carpet the color of Spanish almonds. A sofa, loveseat, and ottoman upholstered in nut-brown suede surrounded a polished teak coffee table. CD's were stacked around an acoustic guitar propped up in a corner.

His quarters even had a balcony. Furnished with two chairs and a small table, nothing more was needed to enjoy the view and the breezes that danced across a brilliant blue sea.

"This looks spacious. Does Captain Rossi share his quarters with anyone?" Evangeline asked Robert, who'd escorted her to Liam's stateroom in awkward silence.

Robert shook his head. "These quarters are larger to ensure the comfort of the ship's executive officers—and their family—when they come aboard."

"Does Captain Rossi have a family?"

"No. I don't believe so." His face reddened as he excused himself to answer a knock on the door.

A brunette in dark blue shorts and a matching polo shirt approached Evangeline with a first aid kit in her hand. In the corridor, a portable massage table and accompanying towels and exotic oils were secured in a wheeled cart.

"Good afternoon, Miss Spencer." The young woman frowned at Evangeline's sunburnt cheeks and raggedy appearance. "Captain Rossi was right. You are a train wreck."

"I'm sorry, but I didn't request spa services," Evangeline apologized, not wishing to inconvenience the ship's staff any more than she had already. "I'm fine, really."

The woman waved her apology aside. "Let's

have a look to make sure. My name is Nita and I'm a spa specialist, here to assist to you in any way. I'm also qualified to change your dressings. Captain Rossi thought you might need some assistance with that, too."

Evangeline stared at the other woman, confused. The last time she checked, she was the prime suspect in a stolen purse investigation. He'd just as soon throw her in the ship's brig.

"I'm sorry. Captain Rossi's orders—no visitors," Robert said to the man standing at the door, demanding to speak to Evangeline.

"Eli!" Evangeline looked at Robert. "Can he come in so we might speak privately?"

Flustered, Robert threw his hands up in a *whatever* gesture, then left.

"Evangeline, are you okay?" Eli rushed to her. His worried gaze took in her windblown appearance.

"Yes. Fortunately I was able to get back on board ship."

"I'm so sorry about this morning, honey," he said, his blue eyes contrite.

She shook her head. "It's okay. Water under the boat." She heaved in a shaky breath. "I need you to do me a favor."

"Anything. Just name it."

She stuck her sea pass in his hand. "I need a fresh change of clothes."

He scowled. "Look, I know you're annoyed with me, and you've got every right to be. But what the hell are you up to?"

"Eli, I'm sweaty, sore, and I'm about hop into the shower *and* get a massage, that's what. Now, stop asking questions and help me. It's the least you can do after this morning's shenanigans."

Eli scrunched a hand through his hair and groaned. "Fine. I'll help. But we need to talk."

"Not this second you don't."

Evangeline watched in dismay as Liam entered his quarters. Tension between the two men sharpened the atmosphere.

Eli bristled under Liam's unrelenting stare. "You can't keep her here against her will."

"Are you here against your will, Evangeline?" Liam prompted.

She shook her head. "Not at all."

"And in case you didn't notice, Buckelew, caring *friend* that you are, she was limping and at the end of her rope, so to speak."

"That's why I'm here," Eli spluttered. "To help!"

"One of the ship's spa specialists is here to help her with her dressings. Give her a couple of hours, then call her suite."

"She'd better be there," Eli warned him and stormed off.

Chapter Eleven

After Liam checked in on Evangeline, he'd gone back on deck to circulate at his party, taking the banter and laughter in stride.

"What's the matter, son? You look none too happy in the limelight as the ship's new pin-up boy," joked the captain, his eyes merry and twinkling in a way that Liam had never noticed before.

Liam blushed like a girl. "Sir, what is the precedence for this?"

"It's obvious there's a romance in bloom aboard the Sea Sapphire." The captain chuckled. "She's unattached, as are you, and she looks like she's close to taking you *out*."

Liam winced.

"Of circulation," amended the captain.

We'll see about that!

Rebellion flared in Liam's crotch. There could only be one resolution to this nonsense. He'd just have to kick Evangeline and her sweet tush *out* of his quarters.

It took another half-hour for the celebration to wind down. Liam dawdled. He needed to gather his thoughts before marching into a demolition derby with Evangeline.

It would take all his military training, his officer training, diplomacy, guts, and a cool head to deal with the lightning strikes he'd endure the second his eyes met hers.

He chatted with passengers and posed for pictures. He helped stack chairs—anything to hold

89

him up before tossing her out and putting her out of his mind completely.

When he returned to his quarters, Liam didn't see her at first, but he knew she was there. His sense of smell dialed in on the rosy trail of her perfume.

Muscles deep in his body strained and tic'd, at war with an excitement that pierced bone deep. Squaring his jaw, he resolved to be hard, even brutal with her.

He followed those delicate floral notes out to the balcony, bracing for battle, even as his miserable body reminded him he was already at her mercy.

And he had yet to lay eyes on her.

She lay sprawled on her stomach on the massage table set up on the balcony. Her face was turned to him, and her eyelids drooped shut. Beyond the edges of the thick white towel tucked around her body, her skin gleamed like satin after being rubbed and scented with exotic oils.

Something tugged at his heart to see her so vulnerable lying there. Harmless.

"Hey there," he greeted softly. So much for leading the charge against the enemy.

Her eyes flew open. "Hi," she said, and arranged herself on her side, clutching the towel close to her body.

"How are you?" Liam pulled up a chair and sat down. The shape of her mouth, her misty blue eyes and the radiance of her skin didn't do wonders for keeping his cock well behaved at the moment.

She covered her pink lips and yawned. "I've had better days. But what a day you've had, hmm? Congratulations on your speedy promotion from ship's engine guy to Action Man."

His cheeks warmed beneath his skin. "I tried to tell you this morning. It wasn't a good time, obviously, but in retrospect, I should have introduced myself properly from day one, Evangeline. This cruise is one of several phases of my new role as captain, but I don't take command until we reach Miami. I'm sorry I allowed you to think that I served in a different capacity."

"It's not all your fault. I drew my own conclusions, Liam. I mean *Captain* Rossi."

"You're free to call me Liam. You're also free to leave."

"Wait, what about the stolen purse? Don't I deserve some form of punishment?"

"Like what?"

"Like a spanking?" she asked, hopeful.

Liam smiled. "We know who the culprit is, and it's not you."

"Will Maisy be punished?"

"I can't discuss that with you, but I promise you everything is going to be all right." He dragged in a breath. "Time for you to go."

She rested her head in the palm of her hand, tucked a corner of her lower lip between her teeth, and stared at him. God help him…how he loved her blue eyes.

"You'd throw me to the crazies waiting at my door?"

If you stay, you're asking for trouble. "One of those crazies thinks he's your fiancé," he said.

She lowered her lashes. "Eli had a memory lapse about that last night. But it's all good. He's on the verge of something special. Just," she sighed and swung upright to sit, "not with me."

The towel shifted. Her high-voltage curves moved around in all sorts of compromising, peekable positions. "And I'm not going to be the one who keeps him from the woman he spent the night with. Your ex-whatever."

"Kerri and I lived together for a couple of years, but it's been over between us for a long time." Liam focused on her toenails, painted a glossy nutmeg color today. "So, everyone else gets what you came on board for."

"It doesn't mean I'm giving up," she declared.

Liam shot up and out of the chair. Aggravated, he stalked to the mini-fridge, grabbed a bottle of water, twisted off the cap, and drank deeply.

"Evangeline," he swung around. She now sat back on the massage table with her legs crossed, swinging them lightly. Her palms lay flat on either side of her thighs. "*Why* are you doing this?"

"Because I want a man in my life."

His snort mocked such neediness. Her eyes widened, then slitted, reading the thoughts behind his reaction. Her legs stopped swinging.

"If I may add my truth to what you've heard about me, Liam…I was married to my second husband for a year. I was his caregiver, the executor of his will, and his friend. He married me to make sure his family didn't rip him off during his illness. And FYI? By year's end, I'll have been alone five years. I'm *done* with alone." Her eyes glinted with frustration. "I'm ready for more."

He battled the urge to take her in his arms, to tell her he understood her desires more so now, but touching her would weaken him. Undermine his ambition. His heart.

Yet he burned like wildfire for her. Still.

"I hear what you're saying, Evangeline. But is it possible you've set your expectations so high for this cruise that they're…unattainable, while other things are," Liam pointed out reasonably.

Her eyes darkened. "I'm aware of your *other* things, Liam. Maybe you're right. Maybe I have been out of touch, hoping to meet a nice guy on a singles' cruise. What was I thinking?"

"But it's not that simple, is it?"

Her cheeks paled. "Okay. So I want the white

picket fence, too. And a man with a job where he'll stay put. A man who'll be there to share in our child's milestones—a man who'll be around to make love to every night, if I want. To know he'll be around for me and not in another part of the world. Or an ocean away. I guess that rules you out, hmmm?"

He winced. She shrugged, letting him know that she accepted her presence in his life wasn't in the cards. He should kick up his heels, but there was no joy in knowing that once she left this room, he might never see her again.

"Why is a man who travels out of the question, for you?" he demanded, perversely curious in spite of his resolve not to get involved with her.

"My first husband had already served six years in the army when that car crash took his life. For much of the time we were dating, then married, he was deployed overseas. Been there, done that, and I'm not going there again." She clamped her hand over the twist of her towel. "I wouldn't expect to be joined at the hip with my next husband, if that's what you're thinking. Just together when it matters."

"Like you and your one-day fiancé?" he taunted.

"There's a man out there who will want me and want the things I have to offer. Like you." Her gaze swept over him, and settled on the erection that chuted his pants.

Liam's jaw knotted. Despite her marriages and that she was so wrong for him, he lusted after her like a crazed bull in a meadow.

"You want me. You just don't want me forever." She shrugged and slid off the massage table with surprising ease, given her bum ankle. "I can live with that." She landed on her good foot.

His gaze scraped hotly over her lips, the points

of her collarbones, the intriguing dips and swells of her body's outline beneath the towel. He met her eyes. "You have no clue how easily I could take you. Use you. Forget about you."

"So I'm just a blip on your radar?"

He wasn't going to lie. "I play for the pleasure of the game. Not the prize."

There—he'd delivered her a last and final warning. One more minute of her limping around in nothing but that towel and he wasn't going to be responsible for his actions.

"May I have a sip?"

Liam walked over to where she stood and handed over the bottle.

Evangeline closed her lips over the rounded tip. Water poured into her mouth, and her throat convulsed as she swallowed.

She linked her gaze with his, handed back the bottle, then took his free hand in hers. She brought it up to where the corner of the towel had been tucked inside the hollow between her breasts.

"Not a good idea," he said roughly, his hand going still. "I'll want more than a sip."

"Take as much as you want."

"You won't get your baby this way." Sharply, he alerted her to the weapons he had at his disposal. "I've got condoms."

Her brows knitted together. "I'm on the pill, too, for now. Please…just don't change the course we're on."

"And afterward? You'll go find some other man to have a life with. Someone to give you that baby, right?" He demanded that she'd commit her future to someone else.

"I want a family. But right now? I need you. So make up your mind." She unwound the towel from her body and stood before him. "Now."

Liam's breath squashed out of his lungs. He

stared, awestruck, at the sight before him: Evangeline naked. No longer the subject of his dreams, but a warm-blooded beauty.

Need kindled in her eyes. She held the towel to her side, prepared to bring it up again if he denied her. Her uncertainty gave her a fragile air that held him hostage to what she wanted.

His gaze swept down her throat to her nipples. Those dusky morsels budded in reaction as he drank in the sight of her breasts. A toned tummy curved along shapely hips. Below her cute innie belly button, a waxed and shaped wisp of hair fluffed around her lush-lipped slit.

His gaze roamed down her legs and paused to study her injured ankle. He winced to see it—bulging, black and blue. He'd have to be gentle with her.

Liam's gaze swept back up and paused once again at the vee of her thighs. A flash of dew glinted through the curls.

His gaze lifted to hers. "You are beautiful, Evangeline."

Relief shuddered from her and Liam welcomed her arms as she embraced him. He swept her up into a kiss of ownership. Possession. Her mouth parted in a warm welcome, and he delighted in the taste of mint, lime, and a touch of the sea on her lips.

The palms she pressed against the back of his neck reminded him that he'd drifted into her web. The sting of knowing there could only be one way out didn't make him stop. No way did he have the strength to throw her out of his room, not when her luscious breasts prodded the front of his uniform.

Liam scooped her up into his arms and carried her to his bed. He lay her down on the mattress, and then stripped out of his clothes, staring at her all the while. Off slipped his briefs.

Her cheeks ripened with a rosy hue. She

squeezed her thighs together as he revealed his muscle-bound limbs to her watchful eyes. "Liam, you're...unreal."

Liam's mouth quirked with pride. He knew what her eyes saw—what he worked like a dog at to keep tight and fit. A smooth chest, hillocked abs, a taut, trim waist...

Her hot gaze flooded him with tingles of appreciation, but it wasn't his washboard abs commanding her fascination. Her eyes drifted low and settled between his thighs.

"You shave your bush?"

He gripped the expanse of his cock in his hand and watched her eyes grow round as he fondled and stroked his lengthening penis. The bluish veins imbedded along its length charged up with lust, mapping out his cock's desire. His hairless, manscaped balls hung heavy. Loaded with heat.

"Sometimes. When I'm bored. Having second thoughts?"

She made a half-gasping, half-laughing sound and her eyes sparkled up at him with humor and delight.

Her smile and the lusty thrill of all they were about to learn from each other made Liam's dick jump inside the bold strokes of his fist.

Watching her watch him pump his cock while she lay naked in his bed made his balls burn. Her breasts bounced softly as she arranged herself on his sheets. His body shivered. To see her nipples, showcased by the dusky halo of her areolas, the slope of her abdomen and how it dipped down into the vee of her waxed mound fed the jerking aggression of his hand.

"You're a wet dream come alive, d'you know that?" The helmet of his cock poked up and mushroomed past the clenched circle made by his thumb and forefinger.

"You have got the most gorgeous nipples," he growled roughly, rubbing his growing rod and savoring the thrill of her stare as he pleasured himself. "I love their reaction to the sound of my voice. Show me how you make yourself *feel*, sweetheart. Rub your clit for me."

He'd planned to shock her by his actions, his words. There could be no doubt. If she wanted him, she'd better know his cock was about to ravish her pussy in a bold, brazen fuck.

He didn't expect that she'd wriggle her ass down on the bed and let her thighs fall wide open. Liam blinked, jolted when her tongue darted out. She licked two fingers, thoroughly moistening them, then brought them to down to her pussy.

She slipped them between her sex lips, rubbed at her juice-soaked knot, and sighed out her pleasure. Her breasts swayed with the motion of her hips as she rocked her lower body, pushing herself into sexual euphoria.

Liam watched, awed by the seduction she wove around them. She moaned and tipped her head back, her hair falling across his pillows as she opened her thighs wider for his viewing pleasure.

"Like this?"

His gaze slitted. "Fuckin' A, honey. Just. Like. That."

She reached up and rolled an engorged nipple with her finger. The finger pad she flicked along her clitoris dragged an earthy groan from her throat and, when she pinched her clit between her thumb and forefinger, wiggling and tugging at that tender bud, Liam moaned.

Gulping chunks of air into his lungs, his hand jerked up and down the length of his cock in lightning-fast strokes while they watched each other pleasuring themselves.

"You're making me crazy," he rasped. "I'll

need to plant my cock inside your sweet, tight hole in about ten seconds if you don't quit."

Splitting her pussy lips wide with both hands, she laid bare to his hungry eyes the rosy core of her. Her blue gaze lifted to his as she slowly dipped a finger inside her cunt.

Liam growled and pumped his cock hard as his desire flared.

She laughed softly. "Ooh, yes. That bad boy of yours will look quite nice in pink—"

"Evie, hush before you make me shoot my load across your sweet little toes."

She reached a hand out to him. Liam took it and raised it to his lips. He caught the drugging scent of her pussy that clung to her fingers, and he darted his tongue out for a taste.

"You're sure about this?" His gaze probed her face, his taste buds abuzz at her spiced honey flavor.

She drew her hand from his and touched her fingers to his chest, to the knolls of muscle that threaded his stomach. Her fingers drifted, lower…and lower still.

"Very sure," she whispered.

His body quivered at the sound of her voice. Evangeline's hand closed over his hand, the one locked around his erection. As her touch tightened, moved, stroked, he closed his eyes and feared some premature explosions would go off.

Liam dragged her hand from his arousal. It was time. He placed his knee up onto the bed next to her. "I—"

The touch of her hand on his thigh cut his sentence short. He simply gave up talking, gathered her up to him, and merged his mouth with the eager warmth of hers.

****

How could such a kiss be only the beginning,

Evangeline wondered, fighting the urge to bite him.

She felt like an *animal*—unable to think. The stroke of his hands, his questing mouth, and the sweep of his tongue spiked her anticipation. Blood frothed through her veins like champagne bubbles in a glass.

The fresh-cut wood notes of his cologne ingrained into cells of memory, forever linked to this moment. His breath sweeping across her skin as he fed on her mouth told her he was creating memories of his own as well.

Excitement seeped from her channel and soaked her thighs. The feel of Liam's elegant fingers rounding over her breast had her hissing in a sharp breath. Total want pulsed deep inside her core when he cupped her breast, squeezed it, and fed her nipple and its surrounding pink lushness into his mouth.

"Yes," Evangeline sighed out through spinning thoughts.

His free hand kneaded her other breast, then his mouth took turns with each one, kissing them between sucks that tore ragged sounds of bliss from her throat. Nerve-endings beneath her skin popped to life against the brushstrokes of his tongue. His fingers.

"Liam," she gasped out his name. The probe of his cock dug against her thigh.

"What do you want, wild thing?" he murmured, dragging his tongue around her nipple.

"To…mmm…ohh…come…"

His warm laugh nuzzled her skin. "Will this help?" He slid down her body and arranged his shoulders between her legs.

She nodded, unable to speak.

"Beautiful." His eyes swept over her pussy. "Just beautiful."

Sweeping a finger between her pussy lips, he

slicked her moisture all around her clitoris, and then lightly touched his tongue tip to the engorged nub.

She moaned. He blew on it, sucked on it, nibbled on her clit ever so delicately. His growl of masculine appreciation buzzed through her plumping clit and threaded straight to her tightly pebbled nipples.

"I could lap at your honeypot all night long," he murmured, then buried his mouth in her sex, rooting out her clit once more with ravenous sucks.

Oh! That could be arranged, Evangeline thought dizzily, but would she survive? When he slid one finger into her sheathe, she arched her hips, her body flaming up with feeling. She lifted her head up off the pillow to watch.

Her hips swiveled. She ground against his mouth and adored how his lashes looked, lowered, as his gaze focused on her gleaming mound, his tongue savoring her taste.

He raised his gaze to hers, his tongue dancing along her clit and pausing now and then to lick across its hood with lazy slides. She hummed out his name when his fingertip wisped over her G-spot.

"Ahh…" She cupped her palm to his head. Clenching her teeth, her fingers dug into his scalp. She held him there and opened her thighs wide as her legs writhed helplessly on the broad shelf of his back.

The harder she clutched at him, the slower he licked.

"Come in my mouth, Evangeline," he commanded, then pursed his lips to the silken hood that cloaked her clit and blew out a tight stream of pressure against its tiny stem.

Her eyes flew open in shock. The sound his mouth made on her pussy was quite…amusing. But the erotic tickle? Out of this world! He did it again to different areas on her clit—around it, on top of it, direct contact with it—resulting in bursts of sensation that heightened her sexual joy.

And when he swept around her sweetly battered clit with swirling licks, she puddled into her orgasm, sinking into the feelings that twisted throughout her legs.

Liam clutched her ass and lifted her pussy up to his mouth. His tongue swept up into her sheathe, only for her walls to squeeze around it with each spectacular contraction.

Evangeline's stomach undulated as her orgasm stormed her body and steeped her in complete surrender. A sigh swept from her lips as Liam's mouth, tongue, and hands took her under and held her there.

He loomed over her, his hard cheekbones flushed and heated. Liam's gaze grilled into hers.

"Ready for my cock, baby?"

His rod probing between her thighs was definitely ready for her! Her whole body quivered with unbearable excitement. She nodded, wordless.

"Hold on, sweetheart." He reached across the pillows, tugged open the bedside drawer, and drew out a foil-wrapped condom. As he fumbled and tore at the packet, the muscles in his upper arms shifted and bunched with power and focus.

When his task was complete, she welcomed the bulk of his body, the strength of his legs, and the rampant cock she cradled in between her thighs.

Chapter Twelve

Naughty blue eyes, smoky with anticipation, gazed up at him.

Liam stroked the back of his hand down her cheek with tenderness.

"You make me wonder," he placed a kiss on her damp collarbone, "what would happen if I did this." He nudged her thighs apart. She clutched at his shoulders when he slid the tip of his cock to the mouth of her pussy.

The puff of her breath stroked the heated ledge of his cheekbones. "Ahh…Liam!"

Her lashes drooped, but Liam would have none of it.

"Look at me, Evie. I want to see those beautiful eyes when my cock slips into you."

Her anxious gaze lifted to his and rounded as he swept the mushroomed head of his penis back and forth over the slick dew that soaked her clit.

"How're we doing, sweetheart?" he whispered, enjoying the eroticism that wove between them as he grazed his cockhead along her folds.

"Mmmmmm…" Perspiration sheened her upper lip. "Good. So very good. So," her lower lip shook, "excited to be with you."

Liam's jaw clenched. His struggle to stay in control evaded him, for his mind and body agonized over her with a hunger that ate through him like acid.

He vowed to do everything in his power to drive her out of her mind before losing himself inside her, but the strength it took to hold back threatened to throw him over the edge, too.

"Put your gorgeous cock inside me, Liam."

He surged into her, going half-crazed to keep from taking her with one solid thrust.

"Evangeline," he groaned, and inched his way into her channel.

Her body devoured his cock. Her labial lips sucked hotly around the roll of his sex. Fearful of causing her pain, Liam withheld several inches of his cock from her opening. "I don't want to hurt you. Your ankle…"

She raised her head up from the pillow to claim his mouth, in a rush to impale his thickness inside her. He gasped. She felt amazing. Hotter, tighter than he'd imagined or dreamed about.

She dragged her lips from his and gazed up at him with eyes a fierce, dark blue. "Balls deep, Liam, *please*! You won't hurt me," she panted.

"Balls deep?" He groaned. Why, yes. Abso-fucking-lutely.

Liam slid the length of his cock into the drenched heart of her. Ecstasy glazed her features. Curls of pleasure created by her pussy's lushness engulfed him.

"Ooh, Liam! Good God—you're large."

The wild orchid massage oil that scented her skin rubbed its silky warmth against his. He could still taste her succulence, how her essence flavored his tongue.

As he rocked his hips and thrust into and out of her with languid strokes, her eyes opened wide. "That feels…ooh!"

The sounds she made! How her body undulated so sensually, so unafraid.

"You move like a woman who loves to fuck," he murmured against her mouth before he sank his cock inside her cunt, to the root.

"Liam…" She wrapped her legs snugly around

103

his waist, allowing his pistoning hips to move freely.

Was she like this with every man? Did it matter, given their arrangement? *No. No, it didn't.*

Her tongue pulsing inside his mouth soothed his conscience. The airtight grip of her pussy gloved around his shaft had the same effect. Doing what any half-sane man would do, he cupped her ass cheeks in his hands and took control.

Liam fucked her with a need so intense it turbocharged the motion of his hips. His cock tickled and ached as she squeezed him deep inside her channel.

The thought that his mattress skills weren't being put to best use came and went. He wanted to give her more foreplay. He'd make it up to her, but being inside this woman right now brought out the caveman in him.

"Yes!"

Not that she seemed to mind. Evangeline circled her hips under him. Her inner walls coaxed each gust and slide of his cock onward. Faster.

"Good Lord! I love fucking you," he murmured, slowing down his hip thrusts to mix things up. He rotated his cock in her pussy with sensuous swizzles, then arched its slickness along her clit.

She gasped.

With his arms cradled under her, he held her close, bonding her to his chest to absorb his cock's pounding quest for relief.

"Hold tight, honey," he warned in a heated rasp.

She clutched at his shoulder, her fingers grabbing at corded muscle to keep her anchored throughout their lusty coupling. Then she reached down and tugged at his balls with her other hand. Hell, that felt great!

He moaned her name against her lips, driven by the piquant edge of sensation her fingers made him feel.

Evangeline cupped his testicles and massaged them, pumping up the tempo of her hips to maximize his desire.

Her snugness launched him into the danger zone, but he wasn't going anywhere. Not without her. He reached between them and lightly flicked her clitoris with the tip of his forefinger.

Busy ravishing her mouth with his tongue and her pussy with his cock, his thoughts faded. They up and gave way to his moans and her sighs. Nothing beyond his door mattered but hitting the peaks of their fevered mating. Raining a series of thrusts inside her sleek passage, he fed her hunger while taking all that she wanted to give.

The power of coming alive between her legs lit his senses and blurred the boundaries between them. Separate dreams? Separate goals? Lines of separation? Pffltt.

She wrenched her mouth from his, her head sinking back into the pillow as she arched her body and threw her legs around his thighs. Her shifting limbs aligned her clit to crest against, and ride, his inches. "Mmm! I love the way you fuck me, Liam."

Liam alternated his hip strokes between wild shafting and rocking his hips back and forth. She gasped and clutched at his hair.

He stopped stroking her clit with his finger and let her pleasure roll through her. The second her orgasm arrowed into her, her features softened with elation.

His entire being trembled to hear his name spill from her lips in an orgasmic flow. Each spasm gripped his cock as her hips pulsed in pleasure.

"That's it, baby," he murmured, loving the quickening of her hips, how her pussy danced over his cock. Her pubic hair scratching against his clean-shaven pelvis added a raw element of sensation to their wild coupling. "Come for me. Come hard."

"Liam—oh…ohh…"

He watched her melt beneath him with passionate eyes. Feeling like a dam about to break beneath raging waters, he bent his head and sucked and savored the pout of her breast as his cock stroked in and out of her pulsing heat.

"Evangeline!" His cum blasted out of him, over and over until he swore his cock would break through the condom.

Liam couldn't get enough of her wetness. Couldn't get enough of her tightness. They kept fucking and he kept creaming until his lust ebbed and floated away.

Finally, he shuddered, spent, on top of her.

A week ago, he couldn't have imagined meeting someone like her. Wanting someone like her—a merry widow, twice over. He'd imagined himself too seasoned to fall victim to shipboard romances. What he'd just done threw all he thought he knew out the window.

"Evangeline," Liam murmured her name and drew her lax body closer to his.

She tucked her head into his shoulder. As he kissed her forehead and breathed in her sweetness, her breath of contentment cooled the sweat that layered his skin.

They didn't have much time left. Given his terms and her requirements, he supposed that was a good thing.

He sighed, regretful. Her body fit neatly in his arms. In his bed. Her mouth—Dear God, her mouth. Its contours had been customized for his lips. His cock. But she didn't fit anywhere else in his life.

His future was set.

His cock stirred, suspended in her languorous warmth—a reminder to make use of what precious time remained. Liam groaned. It meant he was about to fall back into her web.

Then again…had he ever left?

Chapter Thirteen

2015 hours

Evangeline glared at the black leather bustier with its see-through matching harem-style pants.

She never should have bought it but, the moment she laid eyes on it, she'd wanted it. The flesh-toned silk under the see-through fabric ended thigh-high to allow her natural skin to show through. The better to show off her legs.

It was an impulse buy, made the day before she left to go on her cruise. So alluring, its bustier top came attached to sexy, sheer cap sleeves. The better to show off her toned arms.

She'd had to have it and have it she did without thinking of the cost. Much like this afternoon. She should have walked away, but she didn't. Liam had touched her in all the right places, with his hands, his mouth. His tongue.

She shouldn't have moaned so deeply or sighed so hotly, but she did. And later, as they lay with limbs locked and hearts thudding, he shouldn't have said anything, but he did.

This, Evangeline thought as she got dressed, *is what I get for having a one-afternoon stand.*

Like buyer's remorse on the glamorous outfit, she knew what lover's remorse felt like. Her body had been on offer this afternoon, but he'd gotten to her heart.

She slipped her feet into black leather, soft-soled shoes, straightened, and then gazed at her reflection in the full-length mirror. The swelling in her ankle had gone down, too. While it still looked bruised and hurt like hell, she vowed she'd get through the evening, somehow.

The outfit looked flirty and fun and lifted her dampened spirits. She'd gathered her hair up and tamed it into a chic, under-looped ponytail. No longer did it resemble the pillow-tumbled, sexy mess it had been when she'd left Liam's bed.

Oh, Liam! She puffed out an agitated breath. *If only you'd just kept your mouth shut…*

"Unforgettable," he'd murmured against her damp forehead. "Irresistible."

She'd smiled and run lazy hands along his jaw, savoring the rasp of his skin beneath her fingertips. Her body thrummed with satisfaction to hear the contentment that thickened his voice.

"You certainly delivered, Captain Rossi."

His soft laugh bathed her ears. "Gold bars tend to hold quite the seductive sway."

Her fingers stopped roaming. "I didn't have sex with you because of your rank."

"No?"

She'd almost objected when he'd moved away, taking with him their erotic connection. As he'd gathered his clothes, she'd stared at the sculpted vee of his back and resisted the itch to roam her fingers up and down its lean planes.

"I wanted you before I knew who you were, Liam." She'd stressed his name to remind him of their intimacy. How she'd used it to beg him to kiss and lick her in that excitable place between her legs.

"I bent the rules with you on a moonlit deck. You also turned me down when I begged to give you more. But I think I know what this is all about," she'd said. Her body clashed between wanting him and holding back from giving him a swift kick to his outstanding ass.

He'd shrugged into his shirt. "And that is…?"

"Your reminder not to expect more from you than your fabulous cock. Don't worry, I got it. Just don't lump me in with the rank bangers your precious gold bars helped you score before I came along!"

He'd paused and cocked a brow. "Rank bangers? Don't hold back, Evangeline. Tell me what's really on your mind."

On a froth of steam, she'd done what any self-respecting one-afternoon stand would do. She'd climbed out of his bed, gathered her towel up off the floor, wrapped it around her well-sexed body, and limped in search of her clothes.

"Sit down. I'll get your things."

She'd sat on the edge of the bed. Moments later, he'd brought her fresh change of clothes to her, still in the bag that Eli had delivered to Liam's stateroom.

"You realize that other passengers will expect to see you at the captain's dinner tonight?"

"They'll be disappointed."

"No, they won't, Evangeline. You will be there as I'm hosting tonight's table. Especially," his calculating gaze had lowered and zeroed in on her lower lip, "if you expect to see more of my fabulous dick and everything else that *comes* with."

She'd hated herself for accepting the bossy kiss he'd placed on her mouth, tousled with his loving.

"I'm going to take a shower now." As his eyes gleamed with satisfaction, his lips contoured with amusement. "I'll see you tonight."

****

Liam couldn't concentrate.

The butternut and ginger-spiced bisque had been excellent. As was the cuts-like-butter prime rib on his plate, but he had no appetite. He also found the grins that his table guests didn't bother to hide sly and ingratiating at best.

He glanced at the watch on his wrist.

"Have you ever gone rock climbing, Captain Rossi?" An auburn-haired stockbroker in her mid-thirties with a fondness for red wine asked. "You'd love it. All that stretching and muscle use."

"No, but it certainly sounds challenging." Liam's mind thumbed through images of his body stretched along Evangeline's curves, his cock muscling into her tight pussy, and he smiled.

The woman stroked the stem of her wine glass. "It can be intense."

"I'm sure you're right about that." Liam took a sip of his sparkling water.

Then he saw them from across the room— lovely legs that went on for days. A filmy black fabric veiled them as they tiptoed down the floating spiral staircase made of glass and brushed steel.

His heart lurched against his ribs, remembering how those legs had felt wrapped around his waist. His neck.

Liam's gaze ate up the curve of her hips. Hips he'd gripped tightly in his hands. His ears still echoed with the sound of her whimper when he'd finally thrust into her.

Did a hush blanket the room?

She stopped at the base of the staircase and looked around. She ignored his table. Ignored him.

His disbelieving gaze watched as she spotted Eli Buckelew at a nearby table. With a look of puppy dog appeal, Eli pointed to the empty seat next to him.

She shook her head and turned to the seating host as he tripped over himself to get to her. He waved his hand in the direction of the captain's table, where Liam waited.

Where Liam seethed.

She shook her head once more and gave the host a smile full of pleading appeal. The host nodded, turned to Liam, raised his shoulders in a helpless shrug then escorted her to her assigned table.

Eli sat, also ignored, with a look of crushed hope on his face. The seat next to him sat empty. The seat next to Liam sat empty.

Liam's guests, there when this afternoon's drama played out, understood the message she was sending. They all looked over at her unused china, her bone-dry wine glass…and the bouquet of red roses that occupied her chair.

"Perhaps she didn't understand Carlito," offered a member of his wait staff. "I will go remind Miss Spencer a place has been assigned for her here."

Liam did not stop him. She knew damn well she had an invite. He studied the people who occupied her table. Her friend, Maisy, was nowhere to be found. After a discreet inquiry, he was told that she and Mr. Capshaw had ordered a balcony meal service delivered to Maisy's stateroom.

The waiter returned with a message. "Miss Spencer respectfully declines to dine at Captain Rossi's table."

Liam nodded, sipped from his wineglass this time, and smothered his temper beneath the most charming smile he could muster.

****

Evangeline toed her sandals off her feet and climbed into one of several hammocks scattered across the deck.

She gazed up at the serene night sky. Nobody, she thought smugly, would find her here.

"How can it be," wondered a voice out loud, "that we're floating at sea, and we can still smell flowers?"

Evangeline twisted up from the fine mesh roping to peer into the darkness. "Eli?"

"May I join you?"

She nodded and watched him come forward, toting a chair with him, which he parked alongside her before dropping himself into it.

"How are you, Evangeline?"

"Mmm...pretty mad at the world right now. Yourself?"

"Not good. You didn't answer when I knocked on your door earlier."

"Sorry. Didn't feel much like seeing anyone."

"Can we talk about what you saw this morning?"

Since he'd made the effort to look for her, she owed it to him to hear him out. "Sure. Why not?"

He whistled out a breath of relief. "I'm sorry about this morning—about the whole thing. Last night, I'd just left my friend's party and was on my way to my cabin when I ran into Kerri. She'd been having drinks alone at a poolside bar and, like me, she might've had one too many. She asked me to walk her to her cabin. I didn't want her meeting up with someone that might take advantage of her." He laughed at the irony. "So, I made sure she got to her cabin safely, and...well, I won't say I don't know how it happened."

"Then don't. I don't need details."

"Right. Bottom line, I screwed up."

Evangeline shook her head, at a loss for words. What could she say? She'd spent the afternoon in bed with another man.

"I've felt like shit ever since. Believe me, I had every intention of making it an early night so we could go in to George Town together."

"Don't beat yourself up, Eli. I realized as I was hobbling around George Town looking for Maisy that maybe what I came on board to find wasn't meant to be."

"Could this have anything to do with Rossi?

'Cause it was all over the ship—the spectacle between the newly minted captain and the passenger who banished herself to his room. Then, no one saw either of you for several hours. Is it serious?"

Evangeline laughed. "No."

"Do you still want me to court you?"

"Eli, be real! I don't think you really want to marry me."

"Evangeline—"

"I'll be fine. I've got lots of time to have children. And the way I figure it, I met a nice guy— *you*—in a few short days on this cruise. Imagine what'll happen if I give myself more chances like this? Maybe I'll take a Naughty Nautical Singles' Cruise in the spring. Anyway, what about her?"

"Who?"

"Kerri Lorenzo. Is she someone you might want to get to know?"

"Yeah. Right. In our drunken midnight revelations, she said the man she really wants is not interested in her. *Your* Liam."

Evangeline blushed. Liam hadn't been thinking of any other woman while making love to her. That much her body knew.

"Promise me one thing, Evangeline. If you change your mind by the end of the cruise, you'll let me know?"

She smiled. "It was a good offer. Even if you did cheat on me within hours of our almost-engagement."

"Will you have breakfast with me in the morning?" He reached into the hammock to take her hand. "After all, it's Christmas Day."

"Since everything is in shambles, why not?"

He laughed. "You know I'm going to have to chase you now. Right?"

"I couldn't run from a rabid turtle in my

condition."

The sound of footsteps approaching put a stop to their friendly banter. Seeing Liam's hard body decked out in full winter blues—dark trousers, jacket, a crisp white shirt, and a bow tie—launched her heart into overdrive.

Eli stood.

"Mr. Buckelew," Liam greeted crisply. "Are you enjoying yourself?"

"A bit. Evie and I were getting caught up on…ah…current events."

"My apologies for the intrusion. One of your cruise mates is drunk and threatening to jump overboard."

Eli swore. "Where is he?"

"The park balcony, but not to worry. Security has things under control."

"I'll talk to you later!" Eli said to Evangeline as he took off running.

"And *you*…" Liam leaned over her and planted his palms on the hammock above her shoulders so she couldn't escape. Four strips of gold laced each cuff of his jacket and reminded her of his power on this ship. His gaze grilling into hers reminded her of his power over her. "You stood me up."

Evangeline breathed him in, her senses so tuned in to him that she could smell the fine leather he'd lounged on. The jammy richness of the wine he'd sipped lingered on his breath.

"I had other plans," she said, and shrank into the hammock.

"Why?"

"Because I didn't want to show up at your table and be flaunted as the new captain's temporary tail."

"For God's sake, Evie. You left no one in doubt what you were up to when you marched your little ass down to my stateroom! But," he raised his hands in a magnanimous gesture, "while I understand how being seen with me would be an issue for you, we're both unattached, consenting adults. Now, will you meet me in my stateroom later?"

She looked away from him. Her gaze found safety in the stars. "It's not a good idea."

"You don't sound so sure," he drawled.

"That may be true. We both know how much I—" she broke off, fearful she would give too much away.

"How much you…"

"How much I enjoyed this afternoon," she blurted.

"Okay. I enjoyed it, too. Very much. We can have that tonight. Again."

She gritted her teeth. He was so matter of fact. *What's the problem, Evangeline? You want me. I want you. Let's go fuck.*

"No."

"Why not?"

"It was a one-time thing. Remember?"

"We can make it a two, three, or four-time thing."

"Nice that you change the rules as you go, Liam."

"Only if the other player wants to change them, too," he murmured.

Of course she wanted to change the rules! She wanted to ball them up, mash them under her aching foot, and kick the stinking rules right off the starboard bow.

She wanted Liam's touch. His mouth. She burned for his body. His cock. His kisses. His heart.

"Or are you still planning to hook up with Buckelew?"

The deathly softness in his tone made her stop gnawing on her bottom lip.

"And if I was?" she threw at him. Might he be

jealous? "You made it clear that I shouldn't expect more than this afternoon's romp in the sheets with you."

"Evangeline," he gritted, "this *thing* between us may be temporary, but I don't share, sweetheart." He straightened.

"Really?" she stormed back at him.

"You bet," he replied, then deposited a bundle of roses on her stomach. The opal moonlight shining down on them revealed the color of their petals—rich, velvet red. As their meaning dawned on her, it was too late.

Liam had walked away.

Chapter Fourteen

1400 hours
Christmas Day

Evangeline stirred the wooden spoon through the pan of sugar heating up over a low flame.

She felt anything but Christmassy, taking cooking lessons she didn't even sign up for. Once again—thanks to Maisy—she was getting screwed, and not in a good way.

Merry Christmas to me.

"This sugar is taking a while to liquefy, chef," Evangeline said. "Is the heat on too low?"

"Ze heat is perfect. Some sings take time to get right," the renowned Austrian chef assured her.

On board the Sea Sapphire, Chef Johann Dunder was known for his good looks and bad temper.

"What if we turn up the heat?"

"Your sugar vill smoke and burn. Vhy ze rush? Zis is no ten-minute-quickie meal. Pah!"

He shouted out in delight when Liam and the ship's engineering crew strolled into the bistro.

"Aha! Captain Liam Rossi, ladies and gentlemen. At only thirty-seven-years-old, he is ze youngest captain in Jewel Cruise Line's history, and he graces us vis his presence. He'll soon take command of his own vessel. Here is some trivia for you—his father served as Jewel Cruise Line's commodore for many years before he retired."

Cheers went up. The engineers waved hello before helping themselves to the drinks and nibbles laid out for everyone.

Spiced mulled cider, tea, coffee, and eggnog were available, as were small platters of lemon shortbread wedges and cranberry scones, drizzled with a white chocolate glaze.

Liam stopped to greet guests, shake their hands, and take pictures. Arctic eyes and a curt nod he reserved just for Evangeline, and the mental distance he bridged between them chilled the festive atmosphere.

Seated on a bar stool, and without a nearby chair for Evangeline to crawl under, she ignored the amused looks being flashed her way.

She peered down at her sugar crystals, just starting to melt. How she noticed over the swimmy vision caused by her elevated blood pressure, she had no clue.

"Smells sweet in here, chef," said Liam.

"Goot. You stay! Von student needs help. Her partner ran off to be vis someone else."

"Unfortunately, chef, I can't stay."

"Vhy not? Do you have naked vomen in your bed vaiting for you?"

"Not today. Tell you what—my meeting can wait five minutes. How may I be of service?"

"Five minutes to create a masterpiece? Okay. Zer is your partner. You two have met, ja?"

"We've had the pleasure, yes," said Liam drily.

Someone giggled.

Liam took up residence behind her. Did he have to stand so close? His breath brushed her neck.

"Well, well. Alone again," he murmured in her ear. "Fiancé get cold feet in the kitchen, too?"

She ignored him. No point explaining that it was Maisy who'd run off on her this time. She and Eli met earlier that day for a lavish Christmas brunch and, afterward, Evangeline went off alone in search of Maisy.

She found her hiding out in Marshall Capshaw's cabin. Evangeline took her aside and gave her a discreet scolding for bailing on her, and for leaving her holding the bag in the stolen purse caper.

"But things worked out for you, right, Evangeline?" Maisy's gleeful eyes had sparkled like colored snowflakes. "After all, your ship set sail with that fine young Captain Rossi."

"Yeah, well our ship ran aground!"

"What?" Maisy frowned, stamped her foot, and waved her arms around. "What the blazing hell reindeer saddles more can I *do* to—uhh…umm…"

Evangeline stepped back from the woman's erratic behavior. Maisy's choice of words, not so much, but she must have seen Evangeline's eyes round in confusion. Suddenly, as if the older lady waved a magic mental wand, she composed herself.

"Well, that's too bad, my sweet little dear. Was he married, too?"

Now here she was, bamboozled by Maisy into taking a cooking class she had no interest in. To make matters worse, Maisy took off just before the class began.

"Marshall says there's salsa dancing at Neptune's Grotto!"

"That's just flipping great, Maisy," she'd grumped at the older woman and hurriedly took her seat before the crazy chef became too enraged.

She'd given up two hours of her Christmas morning to learn to make caramel sauce when she could have gone to a Christmas deck party, surrounded by single men and cute continental waiters.

And just how *did* Maisy know that Robert was married, she wondered. She certainly hadn't mentioned it.

"Miss Spencer, please explain to Captain Rossi

vat vee are attempting to create," prompted the chef.

Evangeline nodded. "This is a dessert called Plantain Caramella. I am making a caramel sauce to drizzle over these crepes here," she pointed to the platter of crepes rolled up neatly on a warming tray, "which have been filled with braised bananas and cream cheese. These sugar crystals have to heat over a low flame. It seems like I've been here for a while. There's very little melting action, chef."

"Ja, be patient, miss," Chef Dunder retorted. "Stir faster. Harder." Chef guided Liam's hand over Evangeline's, curled around the wooden stir-stick. "Help her, captain."

She trembled at the touch of Liam's fingers. His closeness thrilled her. The thought of those muscles beneath his uniform tensing up as he stood so close turned her spine to jelly. It didn't help that his woodsy cologne called up memories of grazing her lips over his skin.

"Who is steering ze ship, captain?"

"Don't know, chef. Can you go check? I'm busy," Liam replied. When the laughter around them subsided, he added, "Seriously, out on the open sea navigational demands lighten considerably. We go on automatic pilot."

"Tell us about your career," the chef prompted.

"Where to begin? Well, I come from a family of merchant seamen. My Italian father captained cargo ships before moving into the ranks of Jewel Cruise Lines. As a boy, I was fortunate my American mother allowed me to go on sailings with him during my summer breaks from school."

"Which were your favorite ports?" someone else asked.

"All of them," Liam replied. In Evangeline's mind, she could see his diplomatic smile.

"How about a fond memory, then?" asked another foodie.

"An Alaskan cruise," Liam said without a moment's hesitation. "I'd just turned seven. My father and I stood on the deck in the rain and watched humpback whales breach so close to the ship we could hear their breath whistling up through their blowholes."

His tone held such great sentiment Evangeline couldn't keep a lump from forming in her throat. He'd loved the sea since he was a little boy. Someone asked him what he did before joining the cruise lines.

"After I graduated high school, I joined the United States Navy. In time, I earned a commission as an officer on a battleship."

"You didn't wish to retire from military service?" Evangeline asked, burning with curiosity.

"A Navy combat ship differs vastly from a luxury cruise liner." Liam was speaking to the crowd, but she felt his hand pause on the wooden stick. His breath riffled through her hair.

"I much appreciate the responsibilities entrusted to me now—the human element adrift at sea. I'm surrounded by beauty, exotic places, and smiling faces. At sea, a man is tied to nothing—and he thrives on less. Not more."

"Ah. I see the allure," said Evangeline, her pride at not giving in to Liam reinforced, even as her hormones raged angrily at her. Red roses—or blue—their affair would have lasted only as far as the docking berth in Miami. "New places. New faces. No wife, no children."

"Someday I may find a special woman and settle down. Just…not right now."

Chef Dunder came to her rescue before the awkward silence could stretch on. "Ladies and gentlemen, if your sugar has melted to an amber-colored liquid, add ze butter now, and visk. Quickly, quickly!"

Liam reached for the whisk. As he handed it to her, she removed the spoon from the caramelized sugar and accidentally bumped the tip of it against his fingers. He muffled a curse.

"Liam!" Evangeline gasped.

He grabbed a napkin to wipe off the molten syrup, only to find it stuck to his skin like glue.

Chef reached over and dunked Liam's fingers into a nearby glass of water. "Did I forget to mention zat caramelized sugar runs hotter zan boiling vater? If it gets on your skin, it can gif you a bad burn."

"A bad burn, hmm?" Liam gazed down at Evangeline.

"Add your cream *now*," chef barked.

Evangeline ignored him. "Liam, let me look at your hand. Please," she begged, stricken.

"That won't be necessary, Miss Spencer. Happy holidays everyone. Please accept my apologies. Duty calls."

After he strode off with the napkin still stuck to his hand, Evangeline toppled her whipping cream into the melted sugar mixture, and stared glumly at it.

Chef Dunder gave her a look of sympathy and stirred her ingredients for her. "Too bad your captain could not stay for a taste."

"Yes, too bad," said Evangeline.

She took the stir-stick out of the chef's hand. Liam wasn't joking when he said he was done with her.

It was for the best, she told herself, stirring her caramel sauce. The cruise was nearly over and, what was it that Liam had said about one-night stands lasting the length of the voyage?

He'd spelled things out. He'd marked the boundaries, and she'd crossed them by falling in love with him.

****

The elevator moved, uninterrupted, past several decks when it stopped to pick up passengers.

Kerri Lorenzo stepped inside. Recognition crossed the other woman's face.

"What floor?" Evangeline asked.

"Miss Spencer, can we…uh…talk?" The other woman glanced at the covered dish in Evangeline's hands.

What am I? Resident therapist? What were the odds that this woman managed to have some connection to the two men who'd caught Evangeline's eye on this cruise?

She looked at Kerri, ready to dislike her. The other woman no doubt would be as fake as her hair. Instead, her brown-gold eyes gleamed with sincerity and apology.

Evangeline couldn't blame Eli for finding her attractive. She imagined how this woman looked that night, all glammed up and needing someone to talk to. And if the hair was fake—so what?

She smiled. "I'm taking this dessert to my friend, Maisy—the woman who stole your purse. If you don't have a problem with that, you're welcome to walk with me."

Kerri nodded. "Sure. Thank you. I wanted to tell you that I didn't know about you and Eli. I mean, other than the night we met at the club, I didn't know like…you guys were talking marriage and children! But Liam set me straight."

Evangeline shook her head. "He shouldn't have. There were no promises between us. I'd just met Eli, too. We were aiming for something called a *hair-trigger romance*…until you came along."

"I'm sorry. Again. I feel bad about the purse thing. While I don't plan to press charges against your friend, the cruise lines will follow their own policies."

Evangeline frowned. "Why aren't you pressing charges?"

"I got my purse back, and it's Christmas," the other woman shrugged.

"Can I ask you a question?"

"Sure."

"What broke you and Liam up?"

Kerri sighed. "I'd like to blame the sea, but I chose my career over him. I was a newscaster for a TV station in Miami, and he was a bridge officer." Kerri looked thoughtful. "His travel obligations were hard on me, you know? Plus I didn't have the kind of flexibility to join him on cruises all the time. And, when I did, I felt confined after a while. Liam thrives on it. It's the English, Norwegian, and Italian in his blood."

The elevator stopped at Maisy's floor. They stepped out. She didn't tell Kerri that her purse thing was the best thing that ever happened to her on this cruise. It gave her an afternoon in bed with the most exciting man she'd ever known.

Then she wondered if five years down the road she'd be in Kerri's shoes, regretting what could have been.

"So…what about you and Eli?"

Kerri shrugged, but her cheeks filled with color. "Not sure how to handle him yet. He's been avoiding me, that butthole."

"The Sea Sapphire," Evangeline mused. "Ship of fools…"

They looked at each other and laughed.

"Just so you know, I wish all the best for you and Liam."

I wish all the best for Liam, too.

"Thanks. As for Maisy…she has issues."

"I'll say," Kerri snorted. "Let's hope she finds some other kind of therapy that won't land her ass in jail. On the bright side, no more purses have gone missing since you were caught with mine."

Evangeline sighed. "Of course. I'll probably be the one arrested when we arrive in Miami."

They stopped at the door to Maisy's stateroom. Evangeline banged on it. To her surprise, it wasn't closed properly. A pen had rolled onto the carpet and stopped the door from closing. She dislodged the pen and stepped inside.

"Maisy? Hello? It's me."

No answer. She set the dessert platter on a nearby table.

"Hmmm…" Kerri noticed what Evangeline saw right away—two purses sitting side by side on the table.

"Oh, no." Evangeline didn't hesitate to look through them. "I've already been in trouble once over Maisy, and I'm not about to take another hit for her."

The ID's inside confirmed her fears. "These don't belong to her. Dammit, she's stealing again!"

"What should we do?"

"Return them to their owners."

"You mean walk up to an angry woman who has had her purse stolen and say 'excuse me, this must be yours?'" Kerri proposed in disbelief.

Evangeline shook her head. "I have a plan…"

Chapter Fifteen

"Captain Rossi requests your presence in the bridge, Miss Spencer."

Evangeline and Eli were in the Wheelhouse Bar having after-dinner cocktails when Robert approached them.

She glanced at the time on Eli's watch. It was a little past ten o'clock. "I wonder what he wants?"

Eli shrugged his shoulders. "Captain's booty call?"

She stuck her tongue out at him. "Want to come with me?"

He glanced at his watch and said, "Would you look at the time? Can't. Got some packing to do."

"Liar. You said you did most of your packing earlier. Well, fine then."

"Evangeline, don't be like that. It just feels awkward with what happened between me and his ex."

"And have you spoken to Kerri?"

"I will, when I'm back in Wyoming."

She shook her head. "Well that makes perfect sense, Eli, you fool. She seems nice, you know."

"Yeah. Whatever. Anyway, if you don't feel safe with Rossi, then I'll come with you."

"I am safe with him." She sighed and rose. *It's my heart that's in danger, that's all.*

Fifteen minutes later, Evangeline wondered why he called her up to the bridge at all. He'd ignored her for the past fourteen minutes. Meanwhile, he ordered an area safety check of all stations, consulted with officers and staff in person *and* over the ship's communication systems on everything from housekeeping supplies to the ship's football pool!

She whiled away the time and wandered around, finding the bridge a technologically complex and vibrant place to be. Satellite GPS monitors pinpointed the ship's movement. Voices streamed in through radio transmissions.

There were other officers in the low-lit bridge. Two closely studied computer monitors in the cockpit section and another was logging information onto a clipboard form.

When she had the nerve to put her hands on the ship's wheel, Liam snapped, "Don't touch that."

"Sorry." She whipped her hands up and away. "It looks so small," she added lamely, then strolled off. To heck with waiting for an escort! Enough was enough, she fumed, and started to walk out the nearest door.

"Please come here, Evangeline. I have something to show you."

She followed him into a closed-off area that served as a video or surveillance nook. Partially blocked from view, various monitors were built into shelves that showed areas of the ship where cameras had been installed.

She could see passageways, poolside areas, the dining room, and club entryways. Passengers came and went around interior and exterior staircases. Closed circuit TV showed guests milling around chairs and desks in the Guest Services Lounge.

Uh-oh.

"Come closer." He tapped in a date and time on a keyboard.

Shots of herself and Kerri strolling into the lounge flashed across the screen. While Kerri distracted the agent on duty, Evangeline flung a Grand Cayman shopping bag behind the Guest

Services Desk when she thought no one was looking.

"I can explain that."

He nodded. "The shore police will be interested, I'm sure."

"You would have me arrested? Seriously? I didn't break any laws. You don't have any proof that I stole those purses."

"I'll drag Kerri in here if I have to. What the hell is going on?"

She told him how she ran into Kerri on the way to see Maisy. That Maisy wasn't inside her stateroom when they found both purses.

"We thought we'd drop the purses off at Guest Services, rather than confront her about them. Our good deed played out well, too, Liam. The missing bags were returned to their owners with all the cash inside, thanks to the purser who found them inside a shopping bag behind his desk."

"Sounds like you and Kerri have formed a bond over your criminal activity, too," Liam remarked drily. "The three of you have put the cruise line in a precarious position."

"Liam, Maisy needs help. I've been in contact with her son through the internet. I told him everything, just so he's not blindsided when he comes to port to pick her up. I was trying to do the right thing, you know? Return the purses and-and maybe keep Maisy out of trouble."

His brows furrowed. "Even if it doesn't help her and makes you look guilty?"

She nodded. Even if it meant that a man like Liam could never see her as someone he could love. Twice married, twice widowed, and God only knew whatever else he could think of.

"I don't care what people think of me. And for the record, this Christmas cruise has really sucked balls!" Tears swirled up in her throat. Angry, she brushed at a rogue tear that plopped down her cheek.

"For God's sake," he muttered, looking around, presumably, for a tissue. "You should never have gotten involved with that woman."

"She's not all bad. She's lonely." Evangeline poked around the contents of her clutch. She found her travel packet of tissues, pulled one out, and blew her nose. "And I was drawn to her because I know what it's like to be lonely. So if we're done," she sniffled, "I'll go lock myself up in my cabin now."

"And…are you marrying Eli?" he asked, his gaze grim.

"I'm not marrying anyone. I'd need to get to know someone for more than a week to make a decision like that."

"Spend tonight with me."

Her body trembled with want. She shook her head. "You don't know how badly I want to say yes."

Liam gathered her up in his arms. He claimed her mouth with his, stealing away her protests and burying it under his questing tongue. His fingers dug into her shoulders, causing pain. And pleasure.

"Then say yes," he coaxed against her lips.

She inhaled the scent of him, pressing her body against his chest, absorbing its spectacular contours. His body could be hers, his cock *in* her tonight.

It broke her heart to pull back.

"I can't," she whispered. "I want more."

He hauled her up against him for an attack of lusty kisses, but she raised her palms and held them against his chest.

"I need you, Evangeline. Tonight. Damn it, I can't ignore this—whatever it is—between us."

"Sex, Liam. And given enough time and enough sex, you'll forget all about me."

"What the—? Is that how you intend to forget about me?" His arms stiffened, then fell away as her resolve settled into the tension that hovered between them.

She shook her head. "No. I may be twice married and twice widowed, but I've never been loose. I…" she faltered, and sighed. "It's time to move past this."

How it hurt to say the words, but she couldn't tell him the truth. His dream was her nightmare. She'd agonize over him when they weren't together. She'd miss him with every heartbeat, and she'd wonder about other women.

Evangeline had boarded the ship to find a husband. She found love instead and was coming away from her cruise empty-handed on both counts.

Liam breathed tautly, anticipating the hell he was about to feel watching her walk away.

"Evie, I'm about to assume command of my first ship." He clenched his fists to keep from reaching for her.

"And you've worked hard for it. You deserve it."

"Then share it with me. Travel with me. We could see the world together—the Mediterranean, Hawaii, Alaska. The Canaries…"

"What about my job, Liam? My life? Do you realize you've never even asked me what I do?"

He felt his desires slipping from his grasp. What he'd heard, and seen of her, painted the picture of a well-to-do widow with no children to worry about.

"What is it that you do?" he asked, knowing damn well it sounded like the afterthought that it was.

Liam didn't know that much about her, other than he found her irresistible. That he loved her fire and wanted her in his life.

"Never mind. What I do changes nothing."

Harsh truth in that. She'd mentioned being from Portland, Oregon. The cruise lines had a departure port in Seattle for their Alaska cruises and a sales call-center in Portland. Maybe he could visit her there sometime. See where she worked.

It hit him then, the flaw in his dream career. When the everyday cares of guests were cast off for a week or two, he never got to know them. Not their everyday lives, or their dreams.

He greeted them with a smile and ensured their safe passage to ports of adventure. He'd see some them as returning guests. Others he'd never see again.

The reality of never seeing Evangeline again made him realize that his education and maritime training hadn't taught him to say goodbye to a woman he was falling in love with. To say goodbye to a woman who had no plans to change her life to fit into his world.

She gazed into his eyes. "Merry Christmas, Liam," she whispered softly, then turned and walked out the door.

Evangeline made it back to her stateroom on legs that trembled in despair.

She wanted more than a baby. She wanted a family to love, to create cherished memories and holiday traditions with. She wasn't going to get those things sailing the high seas with Liam.

As her dream of finding a husband faded with each nautical mile that brought them closer to Miami, she couldn't wait for the cruise to be over. Couldn't wait for the ship to dock so she could catch her flight back to Portland. Back to the life she knew.

Back to reality.

Chapter Sixteen

Portland, Oregon
Springtime

Liam remained tense at the first bitter sip of his second bottle of beer. He glanced at his watch.

Evangeline was a no-show. And, it shouldn't have taken thirty-seven minutes into the Portland Rose Festival's fireworks kickoff to make him see he'd made a boner of a move.

He shouldn't even be here, not after their last good-bye. What he'd offered her had fallen short of her dreams, and they'd made no promises to see each other again.

That should have been the end of it.

He gazed around the crowded tent set up along Portland's waterfront by Jewel Cruise Line's sales offices. A bar and a buffet offered up a feast for guests to enjoy while having drinks and watching the fireworks display.

What made him think she'd show up, anyway? She hadn't replied to his e-mail. Then again, he hadn't asked for a response. He'd included the time and place to meet when he'd sent it over a week ago, but were the words he'd written enough to get her here?

Evangeline, I thought these past months would bring relief from the memories I carry around of you. Of us. If anything, they're as vivid and sharp as ever.

I'll be in Portland for the Rose Festival's fireworks kickoff. 9:45 p.m. at the waterfront park.

The tent will have Jewel Cruise Line's diamond logo embroidered on the sides. Would love to see you there.

He glanced at the time on his watch again. She wasn't coming. He finished his beer. Time to call it a night.

Liam made his way through the crowd, exited the tent, and stepped out into the drizzly evening.

The river's edge brimmed with spectators watching fireworks sputter up into the night. The sprinkle of raindrops took nothing away from the pyrotechnics, and his gaze was pulled to a thunderous surge of lime-green stars that opened into bright umbrellas overhead.

Watching the sky as he crossed the waterfront, he didn't see the figure cross his path until she bumped into him.

"Excuse me."

Liam's gaze whipped down at the sound of that husky voice. He stared into a familiar pair of sensual blue eyes.

"Hi, Liam."

****

Evangeline gazed up at the man who'd been stalking her dreams. At least, when she could get a decent night's sleep. Even then, her dreams were scorching. They all involved him, her, and one—or both—of them yanking articles of clothing off the other, and doing all sorts of wicked things…

And while she wore a clingy violet-blue wrap-dress cinched at the waist, she suddenly felt the plunge of its daring neckline in Liam's presence.

"Hello, Evangeline."

She stared back at him the way he was staring at her. It couldn't be helped. Her gaze scaled his features, and a rush of heat flooded her limbs with carnal familiarity.

His alpine scent triggered memories of

breathing his essence in when they'd made love in his quarters, how she'd watched him stroke his cock. How he coaxed her to play with her clit while he enjoyed the show.

The lust he commanded made her blood simmer. Her body fought a bone-deep ache to feel him in her arms again. To taste his minty mouth crushed against hers while he pumped his cock between her thighs...

His eyes glittered in response to the flames she was hurling at him. Sparks flew in the look that linked them—sparks that had nothing to do with the pink explosions now blowing up all around them. One of those *booms* broke the intensity of the moment.

"What are you doing here?" she asked, breathless.

"Watching the fireworks. Hoping you'd show. And you?" Liam's gaze probed her features as she struggled to compose her thoughts.

"I come to watch the Rose Festival's fireworks kickoff every year. And to eat a crispy, chewy, floppy elephant ear."

"A what?"

"A circle of pastry dough that's fried, then sprinkled with cinnamon-sugar. My being here had nothing to do with your invitation," she quickly added.

"Ah. So you *did* get my invitation."

"Yes."

"And you decided to take off without meeting me?" He let her know he'd noticed she was headed the opposite direction of the tent.

"That's right."

"Why?"

"Because meeting up with you while you happen to be in town isn't a good idea, Liam. Why are you in Portland, exactly?"

"To look you up," he admitted. "I've missed you. I wanted to see you. How's your ankle?"

She stepped out with her right foot inside her black knee-high, peep-toe boots and used her ankle to draw an O in the air with her toes. "All better. How's your hand?"

Liam smiled and extended the hand that had endured the caramel burn. "Healed."

All he had left to show for a second-degree burn was a patch of white on his finger where an outer layer of skin used to be. "Thanks for asking."

"I'm glad. I never meant to hurt you, Liam."

He reached out and stroked her hair. "Of course you didn't. You couldn't hurt anyone, lovely Evangeline."

She cleared her throat. "So, what else is new?"

A smile drifted across his lips at her let's-get-down-to-business tone. "Actually, I have something for you." Liam glanced around. "Are you here alone?"

She nodded, curious. He had something for her?

"Then there's no reason you and I can't watch the rest of the fireworks together, is there? Like old friends? I promise to behave myself."

Oh, this was cute, especially since *she* didn't want to behave. Especially since she'd changed her mind four times about meeting him tonight. She'd paced the river's edge, stalling, unable to make up her mind. Go inside the tent? Stay away?

In the end, she knew that seeing him would hurt. A *lot*. And marching smack dab into him as she rushed from the waterfront to avoid him struck her as a bit ironic.

Staring into his eyes, her heart pulsed to life. Her body hurt with so much wanting, and he wanted to watch fireworks, like old friends. Well, she didn't do old friends and she wasn't about to start with this one.

"Thinking too hard again, Evangeline?"

"You could be nice and hand over whatever it is you have for me."

Liam didn't hesitate. He reached inside his coat and pulled out an envelope. "Here you go. It's from some people you met on the cruise, but I won't spoil the fun for you."

"I met a darling little kook on that cruise, too." She smiled and took the envelope from him.

Her name was written on the outside in a fancy, feminine scrawl, but she didn't want to open it in front of him. Every moment she lingered put her heart in danger.

"I'd like it if you stayed till after the fireworks, Evangeline. You'd planned to, anyway. Then I'll walk you to your car. Or just walk away. Whatever you want. I don't want you to leave on my account."

She stuffed the envelope in her bag, relieved that one of them could draw boundaries. Too bad she had no intention of hanging around to test them. "It was good seeing you, Liam."

The flicker of his lashes revealed he'd hoped for a different answer. "You're going to miss the grand finale."

"Actually, I never do," she confessed. "I always pick a corner parking spot on the seventh floor of the parking tower. It looks out over the waterfront, and I watch from there. It also helps me get a head start on traffic leaving the area."

"Do you always think ahead?" he asked her with a caressing smile.

"It makes things less complicated. That's all."

"And would I make things more complicated if I walked you to your car?"

"Not at all." She set the pace toward the parking tower, hoping the brisk tempo could shake off her body's awareness of the man strolling next to her.

He didn't have to touch her to make her feel him. She could smell him. His scent found safe harbor in her memory, next to the feel of his naked skin. The memory of how he'd rubbed against her, melted into her when his cock and his tongue slipped inside her at the same time, had warmed her up on rainy Oregon nights.

"So, how long have you lived in Portland?"

She struggled to form a reply. "A-All my life."

"Do you live alone?"

She nodded. "My parents are military retirees. They own a cottage along the northern coast. I umm…have a place outside of town."

A vision of Liam lying naked in her queen-size bed, gazing out at the riverscape beyond her bedroom window, flashed across her thoughts.

"Any siblings?"

She shook her head. "I'm an only child. And you?"

He smiled down at her. "I have one sister. She just graduated college. But since she's single and loves the rent-free comforts of home, she still lives with our parents in San Francisco," he told her with a fond chuckle. "How about you, Evangeline? Are you a single girl living in the city?"

"I wasn't always single, as you know," she reminded him, a blush creeping up her cheeks.

He reached out and grasped her elbow. "You still are, aren't you?"

She jumped at the shock of his fingers, warm and hopeful against her skin.

"I started seeing someone, but it's not anything serious." It wouldn't hurt for Liam to know she didn't just sit around and pine for him.

"Yet you came here tonight. Alone and…wearing that dress. Let's cross, shall we?" he murmured, his breath whispering down her neck as he guided her away from the waterfront. They crossed the grassy parkway to the other side.

Southwest Yamhill was never so thrilling, Evangeline mused. Flutters in her stomach zoomed down her thighs. Liam strolling next to her, asking about all there was to do in Oregon, amped up her rioting senses.

"Let's see…there are wine tastings and fruit picking," she rambled. "Then there is the City of Tillamook on the north coast. The cheese factory there is-is—" She cursed the tremor that shook her voice.

Seeing him again, trying to stay ahead of his lean-legged strides made her draw a blank. All she could see, feel, and think about was getting him naked.

"Is?"

"Amazing."

"Okay."

She had to get away from him—and quick. She was babbling like the village idiot. And when had her knees been taken over by balloons? Her vow to be strong was about to blow. If he so much as came within two feet of her… She walked faster, putting more space between them.

"I don't want to miss the grand finale."

When they reached the elevator of the parking tower, she turned to him. "You don't have to go with me."

"I'll take you all the way, Evangeline."

The elevator doors swayed apart. She stepped inside. Liam stepped in behind her.

They both leaned against the same wall and waited. Fifteen seconds passed. *Whew.* It felt warm in the cube. The seconds ticked on. Was it just her getting hot and sticky around him? Or was it because she'd practically run up Yamhill trying to keep her distance from him?

Why was the elevator taking so long to move?

Don't look at him. Don't…look. She threw a peek over her shoulder.

As he gazed at the opposite wall, she lingered on his profile for an extra second. It might have been two. Or three. Surely it took more than a second to take in all of him—his cover model face, rock-hard shoulders and virile body.

The memory of how his stomach shuddered when she grazed her mouth along that taut path of skin below his belly button leached into her brain. As did his hairless, manscaped balls at the base of his nine-inch cock.

Her peek turned into a stare. She worried her lower lip between her teeth. Her mind spun back to the two of them on his bed, his fingers laced with hers, their mouths joined, their tongues exploring as his cock imbedded deep into her pussy and enjoyed her body with each thrust.

He cleared his throat.

"Evie." He turned to her.

She blinked up at him, hopeful, hesitant. Knowing whatever he asked of her when he shortened her name like that, she'd say *yes*.

"Let me…"

Her areolas tingled into hard discs. She sucked in a breath as he reached out across the space between them…and pressed the button that would take them to the seventh floor.

Evangeline pulled her gaze away and caught her reflection on the opposite wall. A mirrored wall. Crap!

Liam had been staring at her as he'd watched her launch a lusty-eyed attack on his person. She'd eaten him up like a starving she-wolf, and he didn't say a word. Didn't make one move.

She wanted to howl her frustration. The sudden jolt of the elevator made her brace her legs. She felt the moisture of arousal slick her thong, felt its panel cleave to her labial lips. And the smell of him? *Whoa yummy*!

His scent intoxicated her mind with a rampage of hot images. Images she feared she was about to snatch from her mind and stuff into reality.

****

Liam studied her bright, pink cheeks.

Her struggle to hide the longing in her eyes would be laughable if he didn't care so much for her, too. He ached to be with her. Inside her.

He could have just mailed the envelope, but when he received it with a request from the sender to forward, he decided to hand-deliver it himself.

No harm in that, was there?

Big mistake, he thought, standing there trying to keep his cock from springing out of his pants and pinning her to the wall. He had a selfish need to see if she'd found her dream life. To see if she was still available—but for what?

A simple fuck wouldn't do.

The elevator shuddered to a stop. The doors swished open, and Liam hung back as she stepped out. Her hair tumbled down her back in a river of silk. The jounce of her ass under the cling of her dress made him ache to trace the outline of her thong beneath it…with his tongue. He'd follow the straps winging up along her shapely hips. Then he'd trace it right back down to the sweet spot between her legs.

"Coming?" she asked him.

"Yes. Please," he muttered.

She stopped and waited for him. "Did you say something?"

He picked up his pace. "I'm liking the view from here already," he breathed out uneasily.

She turned. He followed, listening to her boots click-clack-clack on the cement floor. Tension framed her shoulders. Liam wondered if she felt the same ache that ground at his gut.

Evangeline pulled her keys out of her purse as they approached a soft-top Jeep painted the same ethereal blue, he realized, as her eyes. It had been backed into a stall for a quick getaway.

He frowned. Unless he convinced her to spend the night with him, her quick getaway meant that she'd be seeing him in her rearview mirror.

She unlocked and opened the driver's side door, and tossed her purse inside.

Then she turned and approached the rail to stare out at the view. The pyrotechnics beyond zoomed into the skyline and filled the night with bells of color.

None of it matched the vibrant beauty of the woman standing at the rail, watching the show.

Liam glanced at the door she'd left hanging open on its hinges and hesitated, cued in to her intent. She planned to leave—without him.

He cleared his throat and shoved his fingers deep inside the pockets of his jeans. "You were right about the view from here—"

She spun around, closed the distance between them, and pulled his head down to hers in a blaze of white-hot need. Her mouth fused into his and lit up the sparks that just needed the scorch of her lips to ignite.

Chapter Seventeen

Liam's scent, the tenor of his voice, his casual chitchat…she barely understood him.

Excited thoughts tumbled around her brain. What was a girl supposed to do with all this hotness in blue jeans following her around? Refusing to let her go?

Get swept away and take him right along with her!

"Mmphht."

Was that Liam or her?

The hands bracing her back to hold her close, to hold her in place for the sexy storm of kisses raining down on her lips—definitely Liam.

He pulled away and rested his chin on her head. His hardened rod mashed up against her stomach. Then again, she wasn't complaining. A minute passed. When their breaths settled, he tilted her face up to his. Hunger darkened the tint of his eyes.

"I take it you've missed me as much as I've missed you, Evie?"

"Maybe," she whispered, then attacked his mouth again.

Liam's laughter muffled against her lips. He pushed her back against the side of the SUV, whispering her name as he did so. His hand caressed her breast through her dress, his touch urgent and searing.

He shoved the fold of fabric covering one breast aside to reveal the lace caps of her demi-bra.

"Someone might see us," she gasped.

"Everyone's watching the fireworks. We're

seven floors up. Hardly anyone on foot here, sweetheart."

He tugged down the top of her bra, dipped his head, and pulled her nipple deep in his mouth. She gulped as a dribble of cream oozed onto the panel of her thong.

Liam lifted his head and gazed down at her as his hand whisked the hem of her dress up. With her heart hammering against her ribcage, she arched her hips against him as his cock catapulted at her pussy, stone-stiff and determined.

She spread her thighs.

"Look at the sky, baby," he instructed, dropping his head to kiss her neck with lips that promised bliss to come. His hand skated across her stomach and swept into her thong.

She shook her head, not about to miss a moment of this. Of him. Of his fingertips gliding between the lobes of her sex. "I don't care about the grand finale. *Ohh…*"

Two fingers slid inside her opening, already sodden. She bit her lip. Dizzy with sensation, she clenched her thighs to prevent her knees from buckling. When his thumb found her clitoris like a bulls-eye, she whimpered.

"It doesn't bother you—" she broke off to suck in a block of air when his digits filled her, stretching her channel with yet a third finger, "that we're in a parking garage?"

His sinful smile brimmed with mischief. "I want to make you come before a car drives down that ramp."

Liam put words to motion when he crouched down before her, his fingers still lodged inside her body. He swept aside the panel of her thong, whistled at the scenery that glistened beneath, and clamped his lips and tongue onto the dampened folds of her sex.

She tilted her head back, her eyes half-closed as his tongue licked her creases, reacquainting himself with her taste.

A gratified sound vibrated from his throat. The warm licks of his tongue fiddling along her folds sent stars bursting across her mind. Fireworks thundered in the sky while her body sank into the pleasure of his mouth nibbling and sucking on her engorged pussy.

"Delicious." His tongue-tip feathered around her clitoris.

He slipped his fingers from her channel, only to dive his tongue into her channel in a thorough sweep before retreating. Then his lips claimed her clit once more with fast, hard sucks.

He left no lobe or ruffle unlicked. Her pussy, clit, lips—everything quivered as Liam explored those supple folds.

Tilting her hips, she rubbed her pelvis against his mouth, thrust her fingers through his hair, and gazed down at the movement of his head between her thighs, awestruck. The energy of his tongue gliding around her slit dragged a groan from her throat.

Her fingertips adored the strands of his hair, threading those glossy locks through her fingers as his head moved between her thighs. She raised a hand and flicked her finger over the tip of her breast, following the butterfly-wing movements he used on her clitoris with his tongue.

Cupping one heavy breast in her hand, she squeezed it, pushed it up, closed her eyes and flickered her tongue out and down upon her nipple. Had he not walked her to her car, she'd never know she was capable of this. Not *this*—licking her nipple, and in a low-lit corner of a parking garage!

But the danger of discovery, this beautiful man nuzzling her pussy... His ears tickled her inner thighs, and her senses galloped toward an explosion.

She seized the moment, using her inner muscles to tighten around the tongue he probed in her sheathe. His finger traced the sides and along the hooded top of her clit, sweeping down to drench his finger with her juices.

The tip of his slickened finger slid to rest at the opening of her ass's rosette.

She shivered. The sensations of his tongue playing at the opening of her core, his finger poised at the entrance to her ass... Anticipation launched goosebumps down her back.

His fingertip hovered there, firm and still against her bud—a question unasked. It intrigued her. Felt damn good too, and he wasn't even moving it around.

He fluffed his tongue under the hood of her clit and lifted his vivid gaze to hers. A pent-up breath streamed from her lungs in desperation. Her breast cradled in her hand, she reached behind her with her other hand and covered his hand with hers, keeping his finger pressed on that delicate whirl of skin.

"I want it," she panted, ready to sink herself onto his finger if he didn't move, and soon. "Give it to me, please."

His tongue slid deep into her pussy, and his drenched finger eased up inside her ass.

"Liam!" she gasped, her mind and body dancing to his finger's rhythm inside her ass. To the familiar strokes of his hands and his wicked tongue. To the growl that thrummed from his throat, a sound sorely missed these past months.

She pumped her hips, sexy glides orchestrated to max out her enjoyment of his skilled tongue. Every move she made heightened the thrills crackling at her core, between her legs, inside her ass.

Liam wiggled his finger around her anal walls, probing her eager depths.

She mewled. He pulled his tongue back and kissed the waxed edges of her mons, buried his nose in the fragrant swath of trim that graced her glistening seam, and inhaled.

"You sure are wet," he whispered, planting yet another appreciative kiss on her mons before snaking his tongue in her cream.

"You sure do like it." She bit her lip.

"I love your taste, baby. Your cocktail tastes *so* good."

God, the things he was saying!

The thrust of her hips welcomed the probe of his lips sorting out her clitoris once more. Liam pursed his lips tight and blew against her swollen sex-bud. The vibration droned against the hooded knot and launched her into a storm of pleasure, movement, and sound.

"Liam…"

He twirled his finger inside her ass. Suddenly he wrenched his mouth from her cunt and hissed in a breath of air. "Evangeline! My finger feels like it's fucking a rosebud. It's so soft."

An unladylike growl escaped her throat. She clenched the ring of her anal muscle around his occupied digit. He chuckled.

"Do you know how badly I want to own that ass?" He dipped his finger deep.

"Yes. Yes, it's yours!"

"And do you have any idea, any idea at *all,* how many times my cock is going to pounce on this pussy?" His lips nuzzled her clit.

"Ooh! Yes, we'll make it a pouncefest, Liam." Evangeline's hands clutched at his head and forced his mouth to make love to her *there*.

"God, yes…mmm…that's—oh *my*! Make me come, Liam. Please, please, *please*…"

He pulled on her clit. She palmed his head and parted her thighs.

Groaning, Liam submitted to her wants, licking and buzzing his lips against her clit. He withdrew his finger from her ass to tickle his fingertip along her anal ring, sodden with excess pussy juices.

Then he stormed her cunt and her senses until her orgasm lit through her limbs in a reckless pleasure burn. Color exploded in her mind, more sensual and vivid than the wildly lit night beyond.

****

Liam could have eaten her for hours.

Her luscious cunt, her ass clenching his finger, her voice, her face, her tea-rose scent all combined to throw his restraint right off the seventh floor.

It made him think things, do things he wouldn't normally do. He wasn't a twenty-year-old sailor turning pleasure dens overseas upside down. World-traveled and educated, he prided himself on his talent in the bedroom. Yet here he was, savoring the feast her pussy offered, his finger vaulted in her ass in a dark corner of a parking garage.

He couldn't resist the downy curls fringing her clit. They tickled his nose, and her nectar… Even as his fingers and tongue dipped and licked at her channel, she kept offering up her essences.

"I could bathe in this, sweetheart," he murmured against her clit. She was so juicy, more so as she came against his fingers. Against the buzz of his lips.

Her tummy quaking with aftershocks, she groaned and pulled back. "I need your cock inside me."

Liam slid his finger from her ass and rose. He licked his lips and wiped at the juices that dampened his chin.

"You've hardly recovered from my mouth, Evie—"

"Liam!"

148

"Condom," he muttered, fumbling around for his wallet.

The rasp of his zipper being dragged down and the sound of a condom packet tearing sent her into a frenzy.

"Hurry," she whispered.

"Okay. I'm ready, honey," he murmured, dipping his head for a lengthy kiss.

"Damn it, Liam. Please shut *up* and make love to me!"

The kiss could wait.

She leaned back against the side of the driver's seat and curled one limber leg up and around his waist to let him know she wasn't screwing around. Her patience for cock had run thin.

He smiled and admired her legs in those long, black boots. She still had her thong on, but now she reached down and tugged the satin aside to flaunt her pussy at him.

"I'm always happy to oblige my beautiful woman." He closed his hand over his cock, angled it, swabbed the head his shaft around her glistening sheathe, and in he went.

She gasped. He groaned. Headlights drifted down from the upper ramp.

"Don't move." He whipped the driver's side door fully open, his hips not missing a pleasurable second to ram himself inside her silken hole.

The car drove by. Liam drove deep, and the open door that blocked the driver's view did nothing to smother the sultry sounds of sex that filled the space around them.

Her fingers clutched at his shoulder, holding fast, holding herself up. Liam held her gaze in his, her eyes half-closed yet hazed with lust, with trust.

And her mouth—that ripe strawberry of a mouth he'd suffered without all these months... It tasted irresistible with hints of the cinnamon-sugar pastry she'd eaten earlier.

"You feel—" she gasped as he pumped inside her sweet, tight vault with lusty strokes, "amazingly big."

"From lack of fucking," he grunted, his length pulsing in and out of her core.

She made a noise, and it was a sound he'd heard before—a throaty, sexy sound. This sound spilled from her lips just as she was about to come.

The muscles in his legs jarred against her inner thighs. Her breasts, with their rose-capped tips framed by the lacework of her bra, made him think of cupcakes in pretty white wrappers. Their fullness bounced with the motion of Liam's cock, plowing in and out of her heat.

"Liam! Oh please…" Her eyes glittered. Her words weren't begging him to give her release. She was already there with the motion of her hips and her body quaking to the tune of his cock.

As he crested into her pussy, he felt the power of her second orgasm roll through her and tremble into the core of him.

"Evangeline," he rumbled out in a ragged burst of emotion. She took his mouth with hers and swirled her tongue into his steamy cavern.

Good Lord. She'd come twice. Quickly. Too quickly—but he looked forward to wearing her out. This was just a warm up.

She tore her mouth from his. "No more, Liam!"

He stilled. "Did I hurt you?"

She shook her head. "No, but now I want you to come."

He slid his cock inside her soaked nest and stayed there. "Mmm, *that* would be nice—"

"On my tits."

He stared into her eyes, bemused. "What do you propose I do with the cock that's already inside you, hmm?"

She licked her lips, reached down, and eased her pussy away from his erection. Then she dropped to her knees in front of him.

He swept the condom away from his penis. Her lips parted and, with a moan, she slipped him into her mouth and compressed her lips over the ridge of his cock. When she gave it a suck, Liam's cock, his body, and his heart melted onto her tongue.

Her fingers dug into his ass cheeks. Liam clutched the doorframe with desperate hands, his head down-bent as he watched her French-kiss his cock with a lush, tonguing intimacy that drove him wild.

"Hot *damn*, baby. I love watching you lick me."

Her hand closed around the base of his dick as she intensified her mouth's suction. She tugged him deep between her lips while her tongue slithered along his pulsing, veined length.

Liam groaned and pushed into her mouth. Her lashes might have screened her eyes from his gaze, but the euphoria that glazed her expression revealed how much she enjoyed pleasuring a man.

His mouth tightened. Giving *him* oral sex. Sucking *his* cock.

"You like licking that cock, don't you, honey?" he murmured.

His thighs flexed as he watched her mouth slide off his shaft, only to pull one testicle between her lips. She gazed up at him, mouthing him with a pressure that launched him into desperate straits. Desperate and drowning in the blue of her gaze.

He closed his eyes when she traded one testicle for the droopy fullness of the other. Sensation grilled through him, blistered with him a need that could only be soothed by her cream.

Suddenly her lips relinquished the suck-hold she had on his balls. When she touched her tongue tip to the bead of pre-cum dotting the eye of his penis, his spinal column threatened to collapse.

"I do, I do," she whispered, then licked up the shiny drop of his cum in a brush-like sweep.

Her breath cooled his glistening rod as she tugged his jeans and briefs further down to fondle his balls.

"Hmm." She paused and looked closely at his hairless pelvis and clean-shaven sac. "Still bored, I see?" She laughed and gave one testicle a tug.

Liam chuckled, unable to forget the grin that stole across her face the first time he'd introduced her to his shaved package. "You have a fondness for hairless balls, if I recall."

Evangeline smiled and licked her tongue around the head of his shaft. Then she gave its tip an adoring kiss that made him clench his ass cheeks and lock his knees.

He wrapped a hand around his cock and aimed it between her lips, lips that parted to accept him as he slid his rod inside her mouth.

She happily tongued the underside of his penis before her lips and inner cheeks pulled him in. Cradling him tight…her mouth moved with erotic fervor, sliding up and down his shaft.

Without a doubt, she loved sucking him as much as he enjoyed being sucked. By *her*.

Liam twined his fingers through her hair. He cradled her head in his other hand as her mouth and fingers gripped, pumped, and coaxed at his cock.

"Sweetheart, I need to—" His words evaporated into a helpless groan.

She nodded and as he withdrew from her mouth, she cupped her breasts—one in each hand— and pillowed them in a delectable invitation.

"Right here." She squeezed her breasts, showing them off, raising one then the other.

Liam's fingers clamped around his penis's

turgid length and he pumped his cock, and hips, in time to his need.

Ecstasy seized him, crashed through him, then streamed from his cock in shots of cream that splashed onto her breasts.

When she stuck out her tongue to taste from his fountain, he spooled out another half-dozen ribbons of cum in hopeless milky blasts till there was nothing left but his groans echoing through the tower.

Liam closed his eyes. His head tipped back in his battle to temper his jagged breaths. Seconds later, delight buzzed through him to feel her tongue cleaning up the glisten of cum that clung to the tip of his penis.

"Oh, *Evie*." He laughed, startled and impressed by this woman he couldn't get enough of. Liam stroked her hair, then drew her up next to him.

"How I've missed you." He sighed, planted a kiss on her forehead and rested his head there for several moments. He laughed again as she rubbed his mess of cream all over her nipples, her breasts, and then tucked them back inside her bra.

"I thoroughly enjoyed that, too."

With sure fingers, he helped smooth the fabric of her dress in place, keeping the connection of his gaze fastened to hers.

"That's not what I said," he drawled and pulled his pants up.

"Liam, you know I don't have to say it. I've missed you. A lot."

"Good, and right now, miss? I want nothing more than to take you to bed and make some serious love to you. If you'd like to join me, of course."

Evangeline buried her face in his throat. "Of course I do," she choked on her admission. *Make some serious love?* What he'd just done to her— what they'd just done—left her body smoking!

153

More than this, *deeper* than this, would fry her to a crisp.

"My hotel is not far from here."

"How long are you here for?"

"Hey, honey." He cupped her face and tilted it up to his. "I know what it cost you to be with me tonight, the fear you've had to let go."

She breathed out a shaky sigh. "How long do I have with you?"

"A week. A month. Whatever you want. I'm off for the next two months and…I want to be with you while I'm here." His Adam's apple bobbed. "You know, see where you live. Where you work."

"So you're not here on business, then?" she asked, curious to know if she was a pit stop for another reason that warranted his visit to Portland.

"My only reason for being here is to see you again, Evie. But if I've come at a bad time…" A look of regret swept into his eyes.

Elation raced through her veins. She wasn't an afterthought. There was also no point in denying…his e-mail had touched her heart, too.

"You're timing is perfect, Liam. But I want you with me while you're visiting." While making it clear she understood the terms, she needed to spell out terms of her own. "As my guest, at my place. My way."

"Your wish is my command, sweetheart." Smiling, he bent to kiss her lips.

Evangeline closed her eyes and swam in the pleasure of his kiss. She'd be a fool not to grab this gift of time with him. Not when he'd gone out of his way to contact her. He'd come to Portland looking for her, and now that they'd reconnected, he was willing to accept her terms. What it meant after all was said and done didn't matter. Not now.

She'd worry about after *later*.

Chapter Eighteen

"Rise and shine, Liam."

Liam woke up to two things—the aroma of Arabica and the feel of silky lips grazing his morning wood. His body hardened as his mind drifted with the ease she took him inside her mouth.

They'd stopped at his hotel so he could pick up his clothes. Unable to resist the temptation of Evangeline being in the same room as a bed, Liam had toppled her down into it and shushed her laughing mouth with his.

Only when he'd plugged his cock into her still drenched pussy did her laughter turn into delicious little sighs.

Now, as she made love to him with her mouth in her bed, the tingle of toothpaste and mouthwash from her freshly scrubbed mouth added piquant dimension. Sensation raced throughout his arousal and spread across his thighs.

With one hand holding his cock at its base, her mouth embraced him with wicked intensity. She squeezed his balls in her fingers, traced the cap of his cock with her tongue-tip, and sipped at the elixir that beaded his slit.

She took each of his balls inside her mouth, rolling those globes around, first one, then the other as she pumped his raging dick inside her fist.

"Mmm!" Liam growled and flexed his hips in counterpoint to her hand. "Hell, that's good, honey."

"You're a very distracting houseguest," she whispered, her tongue glazing his penis until its head belled and bulged beneath her sensual licks.

He groaned. "Bring your sweet pussy over here and I'll give you an even bigger distraction."

She pulled his rigid inches into her mouth. *Suck, tongue-twirl.* When her tongue-tip flurried around his glans, he moaned. *Compress, lick.*

Excitement bombarded him from all sides, even as its aroused core lay in his cock rooting inside her sweet mouth. Her hands swept all around his thighs and stroked his penis.

Soft sighs caressed his ears. Goosebumps popped up his hairless follicles at the sound. And that mouth of hers! He palmed her head.

"Evangeline," he rasped. "I need to fuck you."

His hips rocked and writhed, his cock at the mercy of her sinful tongue.

Gently, she pulled her mouth off his shaft. "No. This is for you. Just for you, Liam, because I know how much you enjoy this." *Lick.* "So whenever you're ready, you can start fucking my mouth." *Tongue-twirl.*

A blowjob? *I'll take it!* Liam ground his hips. As his head sank back into the pillow, his shoulders, torso, ass, and limbs rode high on the erotic roller coaster of Evangeline's mouth.

Her tongue served as the rails, controlling the peaks and falls of his pleasured cock. Wicked hands gripped his hips hard to keep his thrashing ass still.

Liam felt her smile. He used her mouth with shameless abandon while her hands clutched his ass and held on for dear life. When his passion spilled recklessly between her lips, euphoria whipped through his body like a windstorm.

"Ahh!" Liam lost control, happy to give it all to her. She fed on him, licked him up, *devoured* him until he was spent.

"Oh, sweetheart," he said with a hopeless laugh. He would always be, he feared, hard around her. He caressed her cheek, then nudged her up. "I love being with you, you know that? The things you make me feel...mmm!"

"I feel the same way." She smiled as she slinked up beside him on the bed.

He chuckled. "Yes, you've made that obvious. I'm yours to command. Today. Tomorrow. The day after—why is it still pitch black outside?" he wondered, palming her breast.

"Because you're mine to command." She pulled away from him with a soft laugh, taking away his heaven.

She slipped into a robe. "Shower's that-away, Liam."

"Cock's this-away." He pointed to his naked missile, already poking straight up, ready to fire.

She gazed at him with open adoration, barely hiding a smile he found both sexy, and shy.

"You can give me directions later. Don't be long. I don't want to be late."

"Late for what?" He reached out to her.

"It's a surprise," she said, her smile playful.

"I love surprises," he cooed, which made her laugh, and Liam felt the sun shine in the darkened room.

****

"Evangeline, he's a slacker. I can tell just by looking at him. He might be *hawtt*, but...he just screams slacker."

They were back in downtown Portland on the ground level of an older building equipped with a large kitchen and half a dozen picnic tables. The morning sun radiated through tinted windows that looked out into the traffic of the city.

Evangeline laughed. "Can you tell, Gwenn?" she said to her kitchen supervisor, a beautiful, cocoa-skinned girl barely out of her teens. "We'll just have to put him to work, won't we?"

157

Gwenn had slung an apron around Liam's waist, jerked it tight, stuck some steel tongs in his hand, then slapped his ass.

That was his introduction to whatever task he'd been assigned. *This* was his special surprise, and surprised he was when Evangeline unlocked the doors to Morning Glory, a breakfast kitchen that she managed. A place free to the city's homeless and hungry.

"I'll take it easy on him," Gwenn sassed back, flinging steaming biscuits off a baking pan and into a large basket lined with a red-checkered gingham cloth. "Don't just stand there looking hot, Lars. Flip the bacon over before it burns! How's that for easy, Eve?"

"It's Liam, Gwenn." Evangeline grinned at him from across the room, where she was covering tables with pretty matching red and white gingham tablecloths.

She stifled a giggle behind her hand, then made a pinching motion with her fingers, a reminder for him to turn the bacon over that sizzled on the grill next to him.

He pointed to his chest. *Me?*

She nodded, winked, and swathed her lips with her tongue until they were nice and glossy, promising a treat.

By mornings end, he was a bacon-flipping fool.

Gwenn was kind enough to give him a ten-minute break from the grill to help Evangeline bus tables.

"I like your surprise," Liam said as he cleared the table next to the one Evangeline was setting, to make room for the next wave of guests.

She greeted several faces that walked in the door. *Hello, Zack. How's the job search coming along? Tadpole, you forgot your glasses when you came in the last time.*

A family of four walked in. The father, scruffy and unshaven, sensed that Evangeline was in charge. He responded to her welcoming smile, and something blossomed in Liam's heart to feel her care and concern for others.

She didn't ask questions and waved them over to Liam's table to keep the family seated together. Liam shook the man's hand, introduced himself to the wife, and shook her hand. Their teen boys kept their faces downcast.

"Hey, nice kicks, guys," Liam complimented them on their sneakers. He asked if they were the same brand worn by a rising-star basketball player who'd had some hard knocks in life.

His interest in them raised the boys' animation levels and coaxed them to smile. They were soon talking with Liam about the star's latest stats.

"So this is what you do?" Liam murmured in Evangeline's ear when he got her alone, next to the industrial-sized coffee pots.

She unwrapped a stack of paper doilies. "In addition to managing the Spencer Foundation—yes."

"Do you also serve lunch and dinner here?"

Her eyes glinted at him with curiosity. "In the winter months, I serve up soup bread bowls and a simple salad for lunch. It's a little operation, but it fills hungry stomachs."

"I love that this is what you do, and somehow…I'm not at all surprised. But Evie, wouldn't the lovely Gwenn know college students or other responsible people who can help her hold down the fort so that sometimes you *can* travel?" he asked hopefully.

"Oh, Liam!" she beamed up at him. "I can pretty much manage the charitable foundation from anywhere, as long as I have a computer. As for Morning Glory, I can travel with Gwenn in charge.

She's got street smarts. She's hardworking and brilliant. She also graduated from the school of hard knocks, but…I'm not the kind of boss who dumps responsibility on her crew to go gallivanting."

"Okay. I get that. Now what about the baby?"

"The *what*?"

He lowered his voice. "If you had a baby, who'd help you take care of it when you're here?"

His earnest ramblings tugged a smile from her lips. "Ah, ah, ah. Don't go there, Liam. Together for the moment, remember?"

He nodded, but in his mind's eye he pictured her here with a baby bundled in a sling, nesting against her heart.

He bit his inner cheek. In his mind's eye, the baby tucked in her arms had a thatch of dark hair, like his, poking up from his cocoon.

His? Great. The baby was a boy, now, too.

****

"Liam? Are you okay?" Evangeline asked, exasperated.

A thoughtful look had shaded his features while they were speaking in low, good-humored tones. That, and he was poking around her business about her someday baby.

"I'm good, honey," he told her with a smile. "Too good. Thank you for bringing me here. For letting me be a part of your life. Gotta get back to the bacon. Anything else I can help you with, beautiful?"

She shook her head. "Nothing that I can say out loud right now."

A smile curved his lips. "Then do me a favor and think about where you'd like to eat tonight."

They decided to eat in.

They spent a portion of the afternoon at a local year-round farmer's market shopping for fresh vegetables and pasta. Later that afternoon, as rain pounded on the rooftops, they worked in the kitchen.

He insisted on making his secret recipe for chicken basil spaghetti sauce. After she uncorked a bottle of apple-tart *pinot grigio,* she poured the wine into two glasses, then took a seat on a stool at the granite-topped counter.

"What's behind that Mona Lisa smile?" he inquired, while slipping her apron over his head.

"You know your way around a kitchen," she told him, impressed. Liam in her neon purple apron, standing in front of her stove was raising her body temperature. "And the bedroom." She sipped her wine.

He grinned and jerked his chin toward her living room where a fire snapped in the fireplace. "Wait'll you see what I can do in there." He gave her a wink.

Evangeline shivered at the intimacy behind that wink. "Where'd you learn to cook?" she asked, watching his elegant hands tear up half of an herb-garlic rotisserie chicken.

"My grandfather has a restaurant in Italy. I've also picked things up—special recipes and techniques over the years." He smiled. "You don't get to be a bachelor at my age and not know how to cook."

Especially a confirmed one. She lowered her eyes and sipped her wine again, putting aside the reminder that this time with him wouldn't last forever.

Determined to keep their time together upbeat, she tipped her wineglass to his lips so that he might have a sip, too.

With a handful of torn basil leaves, he then tossed everything in a pot of spicy crushed tomatoes to simmer.

After washing his hands, he swept the apron off

his body. Then he grabbed his glass of wine and a couple of cocktail napkins, gave her a mischievous grin and said, "Let's go check out your fireplace, hmm?"

As he led the way into her living room, excitement ramped up her heartbeat. He stopped on the blue-gray sheepskin rug in front of the fireplace, took a drink of his wine, then placed his glass on the driftwood mantle.

His eyes gleamed when he turned and drew her into his embrace. Tipping her face up to his, he dropped a tender kiss on her lips. Then he held her gaze as he took her glass from her fingers and set it on the mantle.

Heat licked around her body. Those tiny flames had little to do with the logs crackling in the fire, and everything to do with the sexiest guy on the planet easing her down to join him on the sheepskin.

On their knees, they faced each other. Her lungs quivered out a breath.

"We've got fifteen minutes till I have to boil the water for the *gnocchi*. What should we do?" Liam asked innocently.

Evangeline pressed a finger to her chin. "I don't know," she said, mock confused. "Maybe...should we start by taking each other's clothes off?"

"Let's see." His voice, husky and amused, strummed her wants and desires.

Evangeline undid the buttons on his shirt with anxious fingers, reminded of each precious second ticking by. Prying all his buttons free, she swept his shirt off his body. Firelight adored his carved male beauty, as she did.

Mesmerized, she traced her fingertips up and down his chest over his tightly ridged abs. Alerted by the sharpness of his indrawn breath, her eyes lifted to his. Layers of passion and warmth darkened those green depths.

Liam's tongue darted out and swept across his lower lip. Reaching out, he lifted the hem of her tank top and swept it up over her bra, and over her head. Then he tossed it aside.

His gaze drank in the slope of her breasts rising up from white satin cups. Cradling her breasts in his palms, he bent and planted a hot kiss on her neck while rubbing her nipples through the fabric with his thumbs.

Evangeline breathed, dizzied by the torch of his mouth and his thumbs doing magical things to her nipples.

He drew back. His look, edgy and hungry, met hers as his hands slipped behind her back and unsnapped her bra. Off it came, along with her inhibitions.

She hurried to undo the snaps on her jeans. Once free of them, Liam tugged her jeans and panties down her thighs.

"Liam!"

They both toppled over, laughing. He saved her the effort of kicking off her clothes by dragging everything off her legs.

Sheepskin softness met her naked back. It was like falling into a cloud and winding up in heaven with Liam's gaze blazing down her body.

He stood up, wrenched himself out of his jeans, and her body blushed with anticipation to see his cock spring up from his briefs. To see his balls firm up at the sudden draft, as if guarding the luscious heavy cream she'd coax out of them in explosive blasts soon enough.

He drew a condom out of his back pocket and kicked his clothes aside. Then he dropped to his knees on the rug, a lop-sided smile spreading across his lips as he tore the packet and swept the barrier over his cock. Placing his hands under her knees, he drew her legs up until her knees pointed to the ceiling.

Being with Liam was so new, so thrilling, Evangeline couldn't predict or choreograph each sexual encounter. She didn't know how every interlude would play out, whether he'd be tender. Rough. What he liked, all his favorite positions— well, correction. He adored oral sex, as she did. And Liam, like everything else he did, had mastered the art of being good, *really* good, with his mouth.

One thing she could always count on was Liam giving her a mind and pussy-meltdown of an orgasm, or three.

His appreciative hands skimmed her outer thighs. Grasping her knees, he parted them, exposing her treasures to his wolfish stare.

He then stretched her legs out along either side of his hips, grabbed her ass, dragged her lower body up and swept her legs around his waist. Reaching down between his legs, he grabbed his shaft and aimed the head of his penis at her vulva.

Evangeline arched her back. Her shoulder blades writhed with delight on the sheepskin fur while her waist and hips hovered in the firelight.

Her thighs, locked around Liam's muscle-packed waist, shook from being teased by the knob of his penis hovering around her pussy.

Scooping her ass in his hands, he suspended her in place while he posed and taunted her by pressing his cockhead along her sodden lobes.

"Liam," she groaned, aroused. Needy.

Then he slipped his penis in its lovely entirety inside her sheathe and filled her to the hilt.

Unable to clutch at his shoulders or grab his ass, Evangeline cupped her breasts in her hands and felt them shudder and sway, side effects of having Liam's cock knocking the bottom out of her pussy.

Moaning, she pinched her distended nipples between her thumb and forefinger. So she'd have a few rug burns on her back by morning. Liam, pumping into her so robustly, would have them on his knees before the night was over, too. But ooh, she was enjoying this wild-hot ride!

Once their warring moves found a delectable cadence, he wafted his cock inside her channel in streamlined glides.

"You like that, beautiful?" he murmured. The slap-slap-suck sounds of their bodies mating mingled with the sound of wood crackling in the fireplace.

His hands! His large hands controlled her hips and her ass. He squeezed her flesh, shifting her around like his personal love toy with her thighs clambering over his hips to wrap tighter around his waist, goading him to plant himself balls deep between her legs.

"Liam, yes," she urged, her sexercised body aiming for a carnal implosion she'd never known doing sit-ups!

"I'm gonna blow, honey. Are you close?"

She brought her finger up to her mouth and sucked on it while keeping her other hand braced on one bouncing tit. After drenching that finger with her saliva, she reached down and slid it between her pussy lips.

"Whenever you're ready, lover," she gasped as her finger imposed self-loving rubs to her clit.

His cock shimmied inside her walls, filling her with rapture while she catered to her clitoris.

When Liam's movements harshened, she flicked her fingertip back and forth across her bud. Its peak bobbed under her fingers, thanks to his cock storming in and out of her sheathe.

"Let me finish you off with my mouth, sweetheart." His suggestion delighted her ears.

"Just…aargh…" His pecs and abdominals shuddered, battling for control. Aching for release.

Evangeline wiggled her hips, wanting him to lose it.

"Woman, you're driving me crazy."

"Then you drive," she goaded him with a whisper, and swirled her pussy around him.

His cock slammed home. His shoulders and spine quaked, each twist of his muscles driven to pour his essence where it belonged—between her legs. In the furthest reaches of her heat where he was free to plant his cock, root and live, forever and a day.

His jaw knotted. Her ears bathed in his torrential groans. She listened to—and loved—the gritty sounds of her man, ready to surrender his soul to the orgasm she was about to give him.

Evangeline stopped playing with her clitoris. She held back her own release, finding it incredibly hot to watch Liam careen into his sexual peak.

Lust flamed his cheekbones. The groans that rumbled across his chest kept her mind and her body fevered, worked up and eager to explode.

"What am I going to do with you, pretty one?" he panted, plunging his inches in and out of her channel.

She gasped. For a split second she thought he said "without" you. She clenched her pussy around him to make him think on it, and think hard.

With or without me? That's your dilemma, Liam, because I'm crazy in love with you, and that's never going to change.

Liam couldn't close his eyes to the sight of her pinching her nipple. Unbearably aroused, his cock delivered a pay load. Jets of cum spurted into the condom as her pussy swallowed all nine inches of him, whole. Her groans threaded with the grunts that spilled from his mouth.

His climax fading, his cock jolted inside her body one last time.

Expelling a long sigh, his satisfied gaze drifted all over her body, her peaches and cream skin aglow in the firelight. *What indeed was he going to do with her?*

He studied her hair, mussed from being swept around on the sheepskin. His gaze inched down to her breasts, cradled in her palms.

His fascination roamed south to the mist of perspiration that dappled her tummy, and onward to her freshly-fucked pussy. To the lips that framed his cock, glazed with her pussy's juices, and still rooted inside her.

He'd figure something out. No way could he let her go a second time.

"Damn, honey," he murmured. "I wish I could take a picture."

Evangeline laughed, and when he muscled his cock inside the condom to flutter against her cervix, she sighed.

The exquisite feeling of having been inside her, of having experienced a ball-busting climax with a woman who occupied his dreams, filled him with an urgency to make her come.

He reached between her legs and brushed a finger gently across her clit's swollen peak. "So lovely," he murmured.

"Aah!"

He slipped out of her dew and gently settled her down on the sheepskin cloud.

She closed her eyes and stroked her breasts, keeping herself entertained while Liam removed the condom. After setting it aside, he turned to his woman and surveyed her with satisfaction.

Her breasts—mmm! Sweet perfection. Their fullness had stuffed his hands nicely. While he longed for another mouthful, his taste buds craved the flavors of her well-loved pussy.

Parting her thighs, he crawled between her legs and dove for the plush lips whose floss of hair glistened with an invite for him to nibble and mouth her until she screamed.

"Mmm…oh *damn*!" she cried as his tongue landed with scientific precision on her clit.

High-octane fueled his blood, watching her legs and abdomen quake with surprise. Her pelvis bucked beneath the suckling tugs of his mouth and he clutched her ass in his hands to hold her down.

She whimpered. He lapped around her clit's hood. She gasped.

Liam glanced up from between her legs and met the stunned look in her eyes. His gaze locking on hers, he pursed his lips firmly around her clitoris and blew out a lengthy buzz along her clit-stem.

"Oh God, Liam. Yes, ooh…make me come!" she cried. Her lashes fanned down across her cheekbones as her eyes rolled back in total bliss.

Liam's fingers dug into the flare of her hips. He hung on for dear life while she toppled into her orgasm, jerking her hips like a wildcat against his mouth.

He licked at her clit-bud, gave it a tender suck, then tasted her flow of juices that coated his tongue. While her hips churned, he hummed, finding it a treat to taste her as she came. To feel her flesh soften and drench his lips with a creamy infusion of her desire.

"Liam…" His name whispered from her lips at the tail end of her climax. Then she laughed and gave his hair a light tug, while his hands and fingers massaged her ass.

Moments later, he was spooning her up against him, his ears in heaven as he listened to the gratified sounds sighing from her throat. Her heartbeats thrummed through her body, and Liam felt each beat above his heart as if it were his own.

Feelings of protectiveness and tenderness toward the woman cuddled in his arms consumed his senses in a way he'd never experienced. Content, he kissed the top of her head, buried his face in her soft fluff of hair, and smiled.

Chapter Nineteen

Their meal never got eaten. The stove had long since been turned off in favor of sating their sexual appetites.

Evangeline lay on her stomach on the furry rug, feeling wonderfully wrecked yet starved for more. Liam left her to dispose of the condom in the master bath. A minute later, she heard a stream of water pounding into her whirlpool tub.

"Oh E-vie…"

She smiled. Her imagination stirred. What was he up to now? she wondered, even as the sound of his voice was enough to get her body snapping with anticipation.

Her veins swelled with a surge of want, even after he'd made her come with his mouth. She rolled onto her side to greet him as he snuggled up to her, naked.

Her gaze feasted on his skin, shaded to gold from the firelight. She adored him, and it blew her mind that he'd come to Portland to be with her. Need spiraled up inside her as Liam pressed his lips to hers, caressing her mouth with his, sharing need and giving warmth.

"Since I made such a mess of you, the least I can do is clean you up," he murmured and drew her up against him.

He carried her into the master bath, his powerful arms managing her as if she weighed no more than a kitten. She was no string bean either, not with her size ten hips and C cup breasts, but Liam swung her around like any capable fireman.

The textured walls, faux-painted in eggshell and rust, gleamed with the flicker of candles that he'd lit and placed around the ledge of her corner tub, along with a condom.

He climbed the rough, stone stairs that fanned out around the tub. Then he took one careful step at a time down into the bubble-filled water.

She sniffed and giggled. "You used rose-scented bubble bath in here."

He kissed her lips. "I love the way you smell. Your skin and your warmth welcome me into your body. Your life. Your home."

He set her on her feet where they stood on the steps of the tub, gazing into each other's eyes.

"Then I wonder why no man shares all of this with you...and I realize," his thumb rubbed her chin, "you don't need a man. And that scares me."

She reached out a hand and circled his wrist. "You're wrong. I do need a man, but not just any man. I need you."

Liam cupped her face in his hands. "I'm all yours, sweetheart..."

She took the next step down and drew him along with her. Together, they sank into a cloud of bubbles and lost themselves in a steamy, watery world of seduction.

Her legs straddled his hips on the built-in seat, but ignoring his erection as she busied herself soaping him up wasn't the easiest task in the world.

"Slip my cock inside your pussy, gorgeous," he groaned as she swirled the bar of soap around his shoulders, his mountainous chest, sweeping up around his armpits.

She shook her head, even as her clit rubbed happily against his erection. The motion of water, the buoyancy of their submerged bodies intensified the sensual currents playing out between them.

She lifted herself on her knees and reached

down between their bodies to work the soap around his cock. Gently, she lathered his balls and delighted in the movement and bunching of his testicles yielding to her touch. He lifted his ass to guide his cock closer to her pussy—a moving target at the moment.

Evangeline pressed the milky pink bar of soap against the band of muscle between his balls and his ass.

"Uh-hum…" Liam arched a lean brow, enticed by this new bombardment of sensation.

She rubbed that bar of soap suggestively, deviously along that swirl of membrane guarding his anal vault, then linked her lips to his.

Their mouths locked and mated in a thick, lush tonguing that torched up a need to feel Liam use those potent moves inside her pussy. But first…

"Want more?" she murmured against his mouth.

"Hell yeah, sunshine."

Evangeline slid her body lower, till her knees rasped against the stonework at the bottom of the tub. Surrounded by bubbles and working only with the sense of touch, her hand snaked beneath his balls, tracing, exploring…

Once her forefinger isolated his rosebud, she glided the bar of soap against it for a touch of lube. Then she eased her finger into the taut passage of Liam's body.

"Mmpht…baby!"

She smiled at his grunt, and his snugness welcomed her finger's glide with a shiver.

"I love how tight your ass feels, sexy Liam," she teased him, and pushed her finger in.

He groaned.

With her digit anchored in his male hole, she twirled her finger around and gave his inner sanctum a few slick, supple pumps.

"Like," he growled.

Evangeline laughed. The look he gave her glittered with appreciation over the things her finger—and the bar of soap his balls bounced lightly along—made him feel, and say.

Slipping her finger partly out of his ass, she curved her fingertip and lovingly palpated her finger pad around his inner gland—his male sweet spot.

He moaned, helpless against this erotic assault.

"So you like my finger fucking your ass, Liam?" she murmured, happy to see his body squirm.

The reaction her finger wrung from his body was a visual treat of muscled satin, writhing helplessly in her hands. With her finger imbedded in his ass, she rubbed the soap around his balls and his perineum while teasing her finger in and around his male glove.

"I *love* your finger fucking my ass, Evie." Liam strained and bucked with an unchecked appetite for her sinful little tricks.

She rubbed the planked surface of his stomach with her other hand and gave him and impish smile as he huffed and rocked against her touch.

He reached out and tugged at her hair. "Get your ass back up here."

She slid her finger out of his heat and rose from the bubbles. His eyes gleamed, trained on her in awe. Laying a hand on his shoulder, she sank back down into the bubbles and straddled him.

Draping her thighs over the powerful trunks of his, she bent her head and plied his mouth with sinuous dips and waves of her tongue. All this while rubbing his beefy arms and shoulders with the soap she clutched in her other hand.

"Please put me inside you," Liam pleaded, his cheeks flaming with lust, his lips red and damp from her tongue tracing their outline.

She ceased her mouth's suckle on his sultry lower lip. "Get a condom on," she urged.

His tongue stabbed inside her mouth with mischievous aggression. Then he thumbed her nipples with a torturous flicking pattern that had her gasping in confusion over the easy way he took control.

He reached out for the foil packet. Quickly he maneuvered himself out of the water long enough to slip the condom on. Then he sank back down into the bubbles once more and dragged her up against him.

"Keep still, and keep your hands to yourself for a minute," she ordered, more for her benefit than his to help her focus on rubbing the soap into a washcloth without losing it in the bubbles.

Liam laughed, completely ignored her wishes and, as she reached around him to scrub his back with the washcloth, he took the bar of soap and ran it up and down the sides of her body. He took his sweet time, swirling it over and around each hip. She sighed. He circled it around each breast. She groaned.

He kissed her lips, stirring up the drumbeats of her pulse as he swept the bar of soap across her back, then into the peachy cleft of her ass. Reaching down between them, he fiddled a finger around her clitoris and snuck two fingers up from her rear to slip inside her pussy and play.

"Hmm…that feels *wicked* nice."

Liam pressed the bar of soap against her ass, keeping two fingers buried in her pussy while another finger dazzled her clit hood, launching her hips into a churning weapon of lust. His strokes lit a fire between her legs as he sudsed her up.

"I can't wait to slip my cock inside you, sweetheart," he murmured, and pulled his fingers from her pussy only to delve one inside her ass.

Evangeline hummed out a sound of approval when another finger joined in. Liam slid both in effortlessly with the aid of her pussy's cream still clinging to his fingers, and the soap's lubricating qualities.

Her entire body buzzed. The sensations of her clit being pleasured, her ass being stretched and invaded by not one, but two fingers, and Liam tonguing her mouth squeezed voluptuous sounds from her throat.

He chuckled. "You've got such a tight ass."

She blushed and arched on his fingers.

"And you know I want to tap that, right?"

"I promise you will," she whispered, sinking down deep on his fingers.

"Stand up and turn around." He slipped his fingers from her ass and gave one cheek a robust squeeze.

A little smile curled her lips. As she stretched back and away from him, he gazed at her nipples, dripping with bubbles, and his eyes smoldered like a forest on fire.

She rose, turned around obediently, and presented him with her ass.

One by one, Liam lathered up her cheeks, sweeping that bar around each globe. Lazy strokes took him from her ass to her mound, and he swirled his fingers through her pubic hair. Feeling between her legs, he gently pinched her clit.

"Ahh!" she cried out. Her knees wobbled. "Not sure how much longer I can stand, Liam."

"Put me in, baby," he growled out the order and guided her hips with his hands.

She eased her ass down to capture the swollen lip of his cock at the entrance of her pussy.

Liam's fingers didn't miss a beat, and he inserted two digits up her ass and slipped his cock into her sheath till he was firmly imbedded to his balls.

"Liam…yes!"

His moan feathered across her back. With an anxious thrust and a ragged groan, he ravished her core with rapid-fire thrusts.

Bubbles danced around their skin, and their heaving bodies launched mini-waves over the sides of the tub as Liam drove his cock between her thighs.

His free hand slid around to cup and fondle her breast.

"I love the size of these," he murmured, her breast swaying and bouncing in the cradle of his palm as he plundered her treasures. "Play with your clit, darling."

She parted her legs and brought her hand down between her thighs to do his bidding while his cock filled her up, expanded her sheath. How she adored the width of him, too. He widened and stretched her in every way.

While his fingers glided inside her ass, her fingers sailed around her pleasure bud and she rode his cock and fingers like a needy vixen.

Their tub play finally launched her into an orgasm so intense his name fell from her lips in a desperate moan. "Liam…"

"Fuck…"

She tipped her head back. He turned her face with his hand to seize her mouth in a drugging kiss, and together they exploded, bodies writhing in the water.

Blood racing, Evangeline reached back with her arms and held Liam's body against her spine as his pelvis banged against her ass. His cock strained and used her pussy mightily before he came with a series of moans.

Evangeline groaned out her pleasure, and if

their lust echoed off the walls and could be heard by her neighbors, well, she'd try to be quiet next time.

She dragged her mouth from his to drink in a breath as she rode his thrusts, his gifted fingers. Hers rubbed luxuriantly around her clit while his drove in and out of her ass. "*Mmm!*"

She couldn't think. Her thoughts twisted like a buttered pretzel until finally she sank back into his chest. He kissed her lips and cherished her mouth with a lazy rhythm that allowed her to gather her bearings, before murmuring promises of more.

Their hunger for each other didn't stop with them wrapping themselves up into thirsty cotton bathrobes. Drying up merely meant they could climb into bed for more delicious explorations.

Cocooned in her bed, they floated on a cloud of thick, winter-knit sheets. With Liam presiding over her mouth, her breasts, and her pussy with long sweeps and twirls of his tongue, her body soon spiraled out of control.

The finger he assigned to her clit buffeted that little pink knot into a climactic implosion for the third time that night. Aware she was too tender for his cock, he filled her with the lovely slide of his fingers, stroking in and out of her pussy while using his tongue to sweep over and around her clit, her lips…

With Liam nuzzling her treasures, her center overflowed. Ecstasy rippled through her body, leaving her a mindless mess rolling in the depths of a shattering orgasm.

How much is too much, Evangeline wondered as she bathed in the affection Liam showered on her. After she came in his mouth, her pussy all a-quiver, he kissed the top of her pubic bone while she trembled beneath him.

Sidling up to her, Liam rolled her gently on her side and spooned her into his hard contours.

His fingers stroked her shoulders. "Are you okay?"

She smiled, thoughtful. "I've never been more okay in my life, Liam. I'm so glad you're here."

He hugged her close. "Me too, honey."

Shivers slid down her back. Losing all hope of sleep with this stunning man lying next to her, she backed her ass up against his cock.

"Uh, Evie?"

"Hmm?" She loved the feel of his rod lengthening against the curve of her buttock and imagined his cock's network of faint blue veins charging with excitement.

He chuckled softly. "Unless your cunt is willing to take another pounding, you'd better knock it off."

"You didn't come, Liam. I want you to come— in my ass."

Shocked stillness fell over him. Evangeline laughed.

Liam scratched his head in two places, thinking he hadn't heard right. "Aren't you exhausted?"

"Are you?"

He buried his nose in her hair. No. No, he hadn't misunderstood. He wasn't hearing things. His lover was offering him her ass at midnight, on a rainy Portland evening. This after a marathon session of lovemaking that began in front of her fireplace, then moved to her tub, then ended with a bang in her bed.

Or so he thought.

She wriggled against his cock. He rubbed his hardening piece between her cheeks.

"Liam," she purred.

His cock nudged her ass in anticipation.

Her girlie growls, her ass launching invitations at him, the need to imbed his cock inside her succulent ass flared to life in his shaft. Lit him right up. Got him hot to climax—inside her ass.

"You've had a man there before?" he demanded, already jealous and dreading what her answer might be.

She nodded. "My husband—my first husband—took my cherry. And my star."

"And did you like it?"

"I knew *he* liked it, and I liked to please him," she admitted.

Good to know. Liam was determined to make sure she *loved* having his cock in her ass.

She looked over her shoulder at him, her eyes wide. "Liam, I don't have lube."

He shook his head. Brushing her hair aside, he kissed the back of her scented neck. "We can do without it."

He slicked his tongue inside her ear and licked its inner curve. As her shiver resonated through him, he nibbled on her earlobe. "But here's the deal, miss. I have to get you very wet."

He reached around her waist and across her abdomen. Then he dabbled his finger through her pussy lips and chuckled over the moisture that flooded his touch.

"Wet, you mean like that?" she asked him cheekily.

"Just like that." He kissed the tiny pulse that beat where her neck met her shoulder. "I'm going to love making you even wetter, gorgeous." He nipped at her neck before soothing the love bite with a swipe of his tongue.

She turned her head to meet his mouth, only to have his mouth ravish hers and tongue her as his cock pressed against her ass, demanding passage to her body.

He cupped her breast with one hand and eased the other between her thighs. While his greedy fingers trawled through her curls and feathered her

179

clit-stem, he murmured in her ear, "The sounds you make as you move your hips, Evangeline? Gets me so hot."

She circled her ass against his cock.

"So fucking *hot*." His mouth fused to her neck from behind as he sucked on the pulse he'd found there earlier.

With his fingers riffling through her labial lips and stroking her clit, her body's lube seeped from her channel. The feel of her liquid silk streaming past his fingers and her tummy catapulting against his arm wrung an anxious groan from his throat.

"That's so good, honey," he murmured. "You've got plenty of cream to prime your ass."

Liam's senses danced with the scents of rose and sex musk filling the air. Her pussy drenched his hand, inviting the rest of him to come in and bathe.

He brought a third finger to the party in her pussy.

"Enjoying yourself?" she panted under his sweltering gaze.

His lungs shrank on a heavy exhale and every muscle bunched with a brutish need to take her ass and take it *now*.

"I am," he assured her, and sped up the tempo of his fingers.

She moaned.

"I swear my ears orgasm from the sounds you make," Liam confessed. "God, how I love your body. The way your hips flare out to that scrumptious ass of yours? Mmm!"

He gave her breast a squeeze, and his cock slid along her soaked crease. Careful not to penetrate her pussy, he made sure her folds slickened his rod with her juices.

"Liam! I need…"

"I know what you need," he breathed into her ear. "Get on your knees, bend forward, and put your hands on the rail at the head of the bed. Will you do that for me while I get us a condom?"

"Mm-hmm."

Liam fingered her clit before his lips pressed a kiss on her shoulder. Giving her ass a fond pat, he let her go.

Propping himself on an elbow, he stretched out across the mattress and reached for one of three condoms he'd set on the nightstand, next to his side of the bed. Snatching up a packet, he smiled.

His side of the bed. He liked the sound of that.

The sexy slap of her hands curving around the bedrails was surpassed by the sight of her derrière bobbing next to his raised eyebrows when he turned to her.

Speechless, he admired the sensuous view of Evangeline on her knees, her silky body stretched out with her hands clutching the rails, looking so demure while she waited for him.

Thick, sultry lashes framed her tempting blue eyes. He replied to the invitation with a crooked smile as he brought himself up to his knees behind her.

Palming her ass appreciatively, he said, "Evie, you have got the most perfect ass." He gave one cheek a slap so sharp and lively it made his palm sting.

She sucked in a tight breath. "I'm glad you like it."

"I love it." Liam soothed his hand over the reddening globe. "Round and firm," he grabbed each succulent cheek by the handful and squeezed. "It's a work of art, and I want to fuck this beautiful ass."

Evangeline reached back, placed her hand over his hand, and gave her ass a brisk jiggle, much to Liam's amusement. "My ass is all yours, Action Man."

Chapter Twenty

Goosebumps bulleted down Evangeline's back thanks to Liam's hands massaging her flesh. The palm that slipped between her thighs sent excitement licking across her skin. He nudged her legs open while his look sluiced hotly all over her nakedness.

Excitement quaked in her bones. Her eyes drifted closed when his hands parted her ass cheeks to his heated stare.

"*That* is one beautiful ass," he murmured.

He reached under her and brushed his fingers lightly over her mons. Using two fingers on her clitoris, he patterned figure eights around her bud while his other hand caressed her back, her hips, and ass.

Round and round, he rubbed the base of her spine. His touch both soothed and excited, with his palm taking a turn at fondling and smacking each of her cheeks.

Evangeline cooed. Every inch of her skin prickled with desire, and while she felt the hot imprint of his hand spanking her ass, the visual in her mind of her cheeks turning red sent her lust soaring to the skies.

The mattress shifted behind her. She tucked her lower lip between her teeth when Liam started licking the skin along the backs of each thigh while his fingers toyed with her pussy. Blood rushed to her slit.

She trembled, dying to come hard as his fingers swirled dollops of her pussy juices along her perianal band.

Sensation hurtled through her bloodstream while Liam's fingers threaded more juice from her pussy and slicked it around her anal ring.

"Liam, ohh...that feels so nice."

His hands parted her globes and seconds later, a luscious tonguing wetness began to flurry around her tiny hole.

Her head whipped around. Up, down, and side to side, Liam used his tongue to brandish glossy strands of saliva to her little pink pout!

She gaped at the sight of her man's mouth making love to her ass, using his tongue-tip to lick around her ring. Suddenly, he grazed his long middle finger over her clitoris.

She bit her lip from the hot carnality of it.

While his other hand grabbed hold of one cheek, her ass blossomed for attention. She circled her hips, heightening the sizzles his tongue and the moisture seeping from his mouth onto her ass gave her.

His eyelashes fanned down and the want that colored his cheekbones as he tongued her added a sultry eyeful to the tingles sweeping inside her ass and her pussy.

Tremors shuddered through her tummy. When he lapped at her pucker and dipped his tongue inside, elation curved her lips.

He groaned. The sound vibrated up to her cervix, stroked her ears, and the ardent look on his face sent sparks bursting from her eyelashes to the tips of her toes.

She curled her toes, amazed by the feel of his tongue driving into her ass like a small cock. Liam crested it in and out, playing her pout with alluring slides and wiggles that had her grinding her tush in his face for more.

"That feels wonderful, Liam, but...you need to

take my ass soon or else I'm going to—" he traced his finger along her clitoris. "Ahh!"

His fingers fell away from her pussy. The warmth of his face buried in her ass was gone, too. Air wisped around the drips of saliva Liam's mouth left behind.

Raising himself up on his knees, the bed shifted again. Powerful thighs brushed the backs of hers. Evangeline quivered. Her hands tightened around the bed rail.

He stroked the globes of her ass with one hand. Thrills winged up her spine, and the sound of the condom packet tearing hiked up her body temperature.

"Honey," Liam murmured. "Your ass looks so pretty."

She gazed over her shoulder at him with smoky eyes. Her ass and pussy contracted. "Take it all, Liam."

He reached for his shaft. Grasping it in his big hand, he kept up the soothing massage of his other palm on her silken backside. Then he aimed his thickness between her thighs and slid it to the mouth of her pussy.

He swirled the knob of his penis in her juices.

"Liam, please…"

"A few more seconds, sweetie. I'm buttering my piece up with more of you. I swear to you, this is going to feel amazing."

How could Liam making love to her feel anything but? Evangeline mused, eager to help in the lubricating effort by rocking her pussy back and forth along his shaft.

She felt the gel on the condom mix with her body's lube and knew the added measure would be well worth the wait. Anything to enhance his king-sized cock's entry into her ass.

Seconds later, he guided the head of his penis

between her cheeks and used it to circle more lubricant around her ring. "Rub your clit for me, baby."

She reached between her legs and stroked her clit at the precise moment Liam popped the head of his cock in her little pout.

Throaty noises rumbled through her throat. Dormant nerve-endings tensed, then exploded to life.

The musk of their sexes scented the room. Her fingers rubbing her pussy, her ring tensing around his cockhead, the heat of his palm massaging her back—all of it consumed her senses.

"Evie, you're *so* tight, baby. It's killing me to take it easy."

Invigorated by his frazzled groan, she rotated her ass against his shaft, while softly pushing at his cock's startling entry. The effect coaxed another inch of him into her inner sanctum.

Feeling her ring sting pleasurably from the swell of his cock, she hissed in a breath and very gently pushed again.

"Ahh…beautiful, baby. That's it," Liam whispered.

Once her body adjusted to his girth, her channel bloomed to embrace more of him. Exotic feelings radiated around her ass, pussy, and down her thighs.

He growled. "How about you go easy on *me*, woman."

She smiled. Her ass was being taken by the man she loved! And the reality of it was that he'd readied her in the tub, when he'd enticed and relaxed her ring, then fucked her ass with his soapy fingers.

In bed, he'd moistened her body and charmed her mind with his tender words and addictive touch. Without him knowing, he'd fed her hunger for his domination. This possession.

The churning sensations from his girth widening her anal vault, her fingers fondling her clit, his rough breath riding her back—it was all so much. Too much! She bit her lip. Her pussy tightened, anticipating his power. His heat.

She looked over her shoulder. He wasn't even halfway in!

Liam caught the wild look in her eyes. Reaching around her, he rubbed her pussy with melting tenderness. "You'll be able to take me, sweetheart. Trust me on this."

His touch assured and excited her. Feeling her passage embrace another powerful inch of him, she closed her eyes and gasped. "Your cock is filling my ass so perfectly, Liam. I-I *love* it."

He groaned and, removing his fingers from her clit, he landed a hard spank on her ass. "Rub your pussy, beautiful."

His smack radiated on her skin. Her ears tingled from the sound. Her pussy, ultra-responsive to the strokes of her fingers and his cock nesting inside her ass, ignited sparks ready to flare into orgasmic fireworks.

His cock's back and forth slides felt so sexy and wild she braced herself for the orgasm about to hit her at warp speed. While he pulsed his hips, she heard something rustle and felt a light dribble where her anal ring clenched Liam's cock.

Enticed to look, she watched Liam drizzle out the leftover lube from the condom packet where his cock plunged into her rosette. The sensuous dribble of lube, the allure of his cock surging into her ass's succulent bloom made her bite her lip and whimper.

Liam's gaze shimmered over her voluptuous peach bottom. "I'm loving this so much. Your ass feels so soft. So snug."

Evangeline groaned. Her mind and body buffeted with pleasure as she watched Liam's shoulders, chest, and abs engage in a sensual body roll meant to put his *all* into fucking her ass.

She clutched the bed rail with one hand, and sped up her finger strokes to her pussy with her other hand.

"Two fingers *inside*, Evangeline," he murmured the command, his hands clutching her hips. "Now."

She lowered her lashes and eased two fingers inside her sheathe. She gulped, bedazzled by the feel of Liam's cock sliding along the flesh that divided her ass from her cunt. His thickness pulsed through the membrane, and the sinewy feel of shifting flesh tantalized her fingers.

With her fingers thrusting and his cock maxing out her ass with delectable moves—Dear God, how hot was this?

"You feel that, Liam?" she breathed, wide-eyed.

"I do, sweetheart. Your fingers fucking your sweet pussy while I'm inside your tiny ass feels incredibly good."

Liam's sensuous body waves, the gritty sounds exploding from his throat, the joy his cock filled her with, including the rapture her fingers gave herself, made her cry out. "Liam, soon…"

His hands gripped her hips, hard. The sounds that charged from his lips unraveled the tension harboring inside both her chambers.

Evangeline exhaled pent-up breaths. Her fingers slid in and out of her sensate pussy while Liam rocked her world. He fucked her ass at different angles yet remained connected to her body and senses with more than his cock.

His handsome face, flush with passion, thrilled her eyes. The guttural sounds he made delighted her ears. It was *her* body, *her* ass, making him so vocal. And Liam's touch warmed more than her skin.

It reached deep inside her heart.

"Mmm, God yes, Liam. More…more!" Her body opened wide to welcome his cock's delectable ravishment.

"Evie! Your ass is so hot. I-I can't take much more."

Her fingers glided in and out of her pussy. Luscious wet sounds from passionate fucking bounced off the walls and fueled their hunger.

He loomed over her and murmured, "Come with me."

His arm snaked around her waist from behind and he slipped his hand down between hers and into her muff, where he grazed a finger back and forth over her aroused clit.

He lit up her world. Set her soul on fire.

Her spine arched. Her cunt creamed. Her mouth pouted into a rosebud and an earthy sound blew past it as her climax sparkled through her pussy and flamed through her limbs.

Seized in the grip of sexual euphoria, Evangeline cried out his name and moved her body in rhythm to Liam's thrusts.

"Evie…" Her name tore from his throat as his orgasm blasted through him.

He dragged her up against his power-packed chest and, while he shafted lustily in and out of her ass, Evangeline discovered all the answers to life's mysteries in Liam's embrace. In Liam's cock.

Through the barrier of his condom, she felt his cock pulse as cum streamed into the condom's reservoir and tickled her ass.

"How I love fucking you." His declaration tumbled out with his cock's last orgasmic judders. The husky sound of his voice made her final bursts that much more delicious.

"Ahh, fuck *yes*, Evie!" One last shudder whittled the breath from his lungs.

The warmth and magic of just being together after mind-blowing sex stayed its course. Liam brushed her hair aside and planted a kiss to her tickle spot at back of her neck. He laughed, feeling her shiver.

Then he seeded kisses all along her shoulder blades—her skin flushed and silky from his loving.

"Mmm..." he breathed his satisfaction in her ear.

The brush of his lips on her skin, his breath wafting across her pores, her body filled to the brim with his cock *and* her fingers—had her pussy quivering with aftershocks.

Liam wound both arms around her waist and, while he rubbed his jaw between her misty shoulder blades, the throb in her body faded to a sleepy pulse. Fireworks behind her eyes dimmed.

Her hand loosened its grip on the rails while her ass still cradled his cock.

Evangeline's fingers slipped weakly from her vagina, leaving her ass to flutter around Liam's cock without her fingers occupying her slick passage.

While time meant nothing in the bed they shared, the midnight hour had long passed when they finally fell asleep, satisfied, in each other's arms.

****

Evangeline was so exhausted that she didn't hear Liam's ringtone or sense the loss of his body heat until he was already dressed and seated next to the bed, watching her.

She opened her eyes, unnerved by the pressure of his gaze focused so intently on her face.

Moonglow illuminated the room. She blinked and noted his smooth-shaven features. He was also fully dressed. The lack of a smile on his face roused her to immediate alertness.

"I have to go."

Just like that.

And just like that, Evangeline nodded, even as her heart shrank in her chest. Disappointment battered at her insides.

"I'll come back as soon as I can."

She nodded again. Her fingers clutched the blankets, while her heart fought against waves of surprise. "I understand. Please, don't worry about me."

"This is not what I had planned, sweetheart. I swear, I'll be back."

"When?"

"I don't know," he admitted. "Evie, I hate this. You have to know…something came up with the captain scheduled for this cruise. It might only be for a week. It might be longer," he added, grim-faced.

She pressed a finger to his lips, stopping him from saying anymore. "It's okay, Liam. Do what you need to do."

"Will you wait for me?"

Yes. Say *yes*…

"Liam," she shook her head. "I've spent the last five years waiting. Married to a military man who was away in Afghanistan the first year of our marriage, then mourning his death the second year. Being his dad's caregiver through the last year of his life. And then two more years before boarding the Sea Sapphire and finding you. I-I just *hate* waiting," she admitted on a broken sigh.

"Evie, the guy you started seeing before I came back into the picture…"

"Oh Liam! There is no guy. There's been no guy, not since you. And even then, you were never in the picture, remember? Not really. You hadn't written. You never even called."

She swallowed past the heartache that

thickened her throat. Once again, he had to go back to his reality, and she to hers. "I had a life before you, and I'll have a life after you. The truth is, maybe I will wait for you. And maybe I won't. I just can't wait forever."

She was getting good at this, letting men go.

"Fair enough. But damn it...I don't want to leave you! And don't think for one second that these months without you were easy on me. You occupied my thoughts every waking minute, and invaded my dreams at night. That's why I had to come." He reached for her. "Evangeline, I—"

"Go, Liam."

She couldn't bear to hear it. She didn't care if he was about to say *I'm sorry* or even *I love you*. He was still going to leave, and she would still choose to wait.

Chapter Twenty-One

"Beyond these doors lies a feast fit for a king. Foods from all over the world—Greek *gyros* to aged Texas Prime Rib—is yours to indulge." Liam waved the blonde reporter and cameraman past the sliding glass doors.

He strolled with them toward the buffet of the International Bistro—and ignored the interest in the reporter's eyes as her gaze met his.

"Thanks so much for taking the time to give Cruiser News this special tour, Captain Rossi. I must say, I've worked up quite the...umm, appetite." Her look invited him to be the main course.

Liam smiled as his mind filled with thoughts of a meal uneaten. Of the morning he'd had to leave Evangeline three weeks ago.

He hoped she received the cards he'd sent. One for every week he'd been gone. Plus the postcards he'd mailed from every port the ship visited in the Caribbean to keep him fresh in her mind, hoping that she'd wait for him.

"The blood-orange sponge cake torte with Cointreau custard will satisfy any craving you have," he assured the reporter with a smile, anxious to end this tour.

He needed to talk to Evangeline. God knows he'd practiced "the speech" a dozen times. He was going to lay his heart at her high-heeled feet and let her know how much he missed her. That he was willing to change his life. Not just to meet her halfway, but *all* the way.

"Captain Rossi?"

Liam blinked when the reporter's face drifted into focus. Her smile cooling, she said, "Thank you for your time, captain. I take it you have no interest in joining me—us—for this fabulous meal?"

"My apologies. I'm otherwise…committed."

Over the ship's PA system, he was being summoned to the bridge. It couldn't have come at a more perfect time. He excused himself, shook the cameraman's hand, shook the reporter's hand, and then left.

Up in the bridge, Liam answered the call on hold for him. "This is Captain Rossi."

"Is that you, slacker-man?"

"Gwenn?" Only one person called him that. His heart nose-dived into his stomach. "What's wrong?"

"Evangeline doesn't know I'm calling you, but I thought you should know. She's been in an accident."

The world shifted on its axis. Or maybe the ship was simply rocking next to the dock. But for a few seconds, Liam's life as he knew it went for a spin. "What happened?"

He could hear the line crackle. Her voice faded with words he couldn't make out.

"She fell and fractured her…" *crackle-crackle*, "…and then she has a…" *crackle-crackle*, "…but she's on her way to…" *crackle-crackle*, "…but the good news is she's gonna be all right. Take good care of her, ya hear?"

The line went dead.

"Gwenn!" He began dialing the number he'd memorized after practicing "the speech" multiple times.

Wait—*what*? Take good care of her? *What did she mean by that?*

"Everything all right, sir?"

He didn't know which officer spoke to him.

The roar in his ears clashed with the hammering of his heart.

"Uh…Captain Rossi?"

Liam finished dialing.

"Sir—"

Liam threw a hand up and speared his XO with a glare. "I," he gritted, "am attempting to call the love of my life! What is it?"

The first officer grinned as an amused silence stole across the bridge. The officers were all looking in the direction of the exterior doors leading to and from the bridge.

He turned his head and the phone fell out of his hand.

****

Evangeline stood in the open doorway, gazing at him.

Port breezes fluttered her hair and skimmed around her bare legs. Her toes curled inside her electric blue deck shoes. Anxiety clenched at her stomach.

Her right arm, bound and held up in a sling, ached. The stabbing pain caused by the bone spur in her shoulder added to her misery. Of course Liam's rejection would finish her off, but even in pain and with her heart uncertain, she had to come.

She couldn't gauge much from his features, other than her showing up on his ship had come as a surprise. As had been her last minute decision to fly to Miami.

Maybe she needed to clean out her ears, too, but she could have sworn she heard him snap at his crew that he was trying to call the love of his life.

In his white uniform, his gold-barred shoulder-boards framed his aura of command. He looked every inch the ship's commander—professional and unapproachable. At least to her, since she wasn't here on ship's business.

This was personal.

She cleared her throat. "Hi Liam. Is this a good time?"

A dark brow angled up. "I could guarantee you a good time," Liam greeted softly, "but I don't think that's what you're asking. What happened, Evangeline?"

She bit her lip as a full-throttle body blush warmed her from her cheeks to her toes. His gaze glinted with virile interest, and his irresistible words floated along her pulse points.

"I tripped on the sidewalk outside Morning Glory. It was raining, and I slipped in my heels. Fractured my arm. Dislocated my elbow. As I lay there in pain while being rained on at the bottom of the stairwell, I figured the icing on this cake would be to go on a cruise."

Liam grinned. "I can see the logic in that since you're not going to be much help to Gwenn. So you'll be joining us for Kerri and Eli's wedding on Pirate Island?"

"As will Maisy and her family," she happily informed him.

"If so much as a fucking toothpick goes missing...so help me God, Evie, I'll put her ashore at the first port of call. Let's go somewhere we can talk, shall we?"

His gaze skimmed her features and the glow in his eyes promised more than talk. If he could read her mind, he'd have laughed at her only thought. *Can that somewhere include a bed?*

Minutes later, they were nowhere near a bed.

They were in an interior passageway, next to a door that said "No Unauthorized Entry," just outside the ship's engine room, where they first met. He stood away from her, one hand hitched on his lean hip and the other rested along a handrail. His fingers tapped thoughtfully along the curve of the metal.

"Is it just Kerri and Eli's wedding that brings you cross country, Evangeline?"

She gave him a searching look. "Liam, I know this is late in coming…I love you. You asked me three weeks ago if I'd wait. I came to tell you in person, I will."

"You're sure, Evie? Because I tried this once and it didn't work out."

"I'm not Kerri!"

"Thank God," he retorted, which made her smile.

"At least we both want to try, Liam. I lost out with my first husband. I don't want to miss out on you."

"And what about your someday baby-daddy out there?"

She shrugged. "He's just going to have to wait on me 'cause I've got a life to live. With *you*. Your side of the bed will be there, waiting for you." She eased out a small, nervous breath. "I should go—"

"It's too late, Evangeline."

She felt herself sway. "I-I understand. I waited too long."

"You don't understand. It's too late for your somewhere-out-there baby-daddy. That position will be mine."

Her heart turned into a turbo-charged instrument of disbelief.

"Will you be my baby-mama?"

She opened then closed her mouth, lost for words. Yet wanting to laugh at the hip proposal coming from this hot, high-ranking maritime professional, gazing at her with adoration. And love.

"I'll do whatever you want, Evangeline. I'll take a land-based position; a regular nine-to-five office job. I'll—"

"Liam?" Evangeline shook her head, in awe of the delicious hunk laying his heart at her feet. "What's changed? Because I'll be there, you know, for you. For as long as you love me."

Her breath caught at the force of his passion when he reached out and curved both hands around her shoulders.

"What changed for me?" He brushed her skin with silken thumbs, his voice husky as his gaze cherished her face. "I didn't sign up to fall in love with a blue-eyed wench the minute I'd made captain. I was a man on the move and," he hesitated, but admitted, "a long-term relationship wasn't in the cards for me. I'd already had one go south."

Evangeline touched his jaw with her fingertips to let him know she understood his dreams. His conflicts.

"My own ship, my own command—I won't deny it has its perks. But not having you in my life to share the rewards? Not being able to share in *your* life?" He shook his head. "Not going to happen. How many seas do I need to sail, beautiful? I've been all over the world. Traveled many oceans—"

"Bedded many beautiful women."

He chuckled. "You got me there, sunshine. But like you, I want more. I'm so ready for more. I just didn't know what I needed until I met you."

His heartfelt words freed her mind to accept his love. The vision he had for his future held a special place for her after all, right by his side.

"Liam Rossi, if you think we're going to be stuck at home every night like a worn out pair of shoes, you've got another think coming. I also don't plan to let you out of my sight much! If I can travel with you, then I will."

"Oh, you will." His eyes twinkled with

promises. "And we won't always be traveling. I'll be off several months out of the year. I'll be there to help you with Morning Glory—and in every other way. But I don't want you unhappy, to have to travel."

"Oh trust me. I'm pretty miserable when you're *not* around," she whispered, and stepped closer to him. She reached out with her good arm and cupped his balls and cock in her hand. "Hmm. Already hard, I see."

He stifled a groan. "We sail for the Eastern Caribbean at seventeen-hundred hours. You do realize that you're mine, right? No more of this find-a-husband-in-twenty-four-hours bullshit."

"That depends. Are you offering me a holiday, captain?"

"Roses and romance, too." Liam's gaze seared into her eyes. The fire in them kindled with pleasure as he raised his hand and grazed her cheek with his knuckles. Then he bent his head, kissed her lips, and murmured, "An all-inclusive package, baby."

About the Author

Just for fun, Lelani Black used to write motocross articles for a motocross website. One day a sports editor for a national magazine read one of her articles and invited her to submit her articles to them—for money! That one kindness shown to her by an editor gave her the confidence to keep nurturing her passion for writing. Her debut erotic romance, *Boss With Benefits*, was her first foray into her journey as an author of erotic, romantic fiction. It's been full-throttle fun ever since!

Visit Lelani at
http://www.lelaniblack.com

To chat with Lelani Black and other Wild Rose Press authors of erotic romance, join us at www.groups.yahoo.com/group/thewilderroses.

Also Available

Private Dancer

by

Lelani Black

Harrison Allandt aches for his sexy-sweet fiancée to crank up the heat in the bedroom. But as he discovers the startling depths of her sensuality, he can't help but wonder what other secrets this picture-perfect beauty is hiding.

Desperate to keep her bikini boutique from going belly-up and struggling to pay for her grandmother's medical care, Jacinta Carr will risk anything. Even taking the stage as one of Honolulu's hottest pole dancers.

But when Harry finds out, will he walk away or will he name his own price—a private dance?

Chapter One

Harrison Keanu Allandt strode purposefully past the noisy crowd that milled around a brightly lit boutique window near downtown Honolulu's Fort Street Mall. Due back in his office for a client meeting, he hadn't anticipated the business luncheon he was returning from to last an hour longer than he'd expected.

Flashing neon lights, a catchy dance beat followed by movement beyond the glass coaxed a passing glance from him. He turned his head, and the sight that greeted him made him stop, and stare.

Golden-sugar hair rippled down the scantily clad back of a woman, stopping just short of a delectable peach of an ass, now giving the crowd an outrageous shake inside the bottoms of a tiger print, one-piece swimsuit. Harry grinned, impressed by this bold marketing strategy.

Captivated, he watched her strut her sleek, endless legs to a naughty stream of lyrics thumping from a speaker propped against the shop's entrance.

His gaze slid down her incredibly sexy body whose shapely curves promised sizzling nights on cool, silk sheets. As she moved, barefoot in real sand, her ass shimmied in a way that made his tongue tingle for a taste of the juicy flesh hidden inside the clingy fabric.

Sunglasses propped on her head swept her glossy brown hair away from her features.

The better to see your face, my pretty.

She caught his stare on her second sweep across the stage. Harry watched her, intrigued. The feminine outline of her face framed lovely features, with eyebrows that winged above wide-spaced eyes whose color he couldn't immediately define.

As his gaze zoomed in on her mouth, he imagined driving his tongue between those soft lips, certain they'd taste good, too. She blinked, the pace of her dancing thrown off several beats by his bold male assessment.

Harry winked.

Startled, she dropped her bottle of suntan oil.

The rush of pink flooding her cheeks charmed him, along with the awkward pause in her leggy stride.

He stepped forward and pointed to the bottle poking up from the shallow layer of sand. "Aren't you going to pick that up, sweetheart?" he asked through the window, his smile daring her to bend over.

She bit her lip, shook her head, and toed the bottle off to the side. As she hurried off the stage, the men in the crowd groaned with disappointment.

A bare-chested, muscle-ripped male model in volcanic-colored board shorts and black rubber flip-flops—a boogie board slung under his arm—sauntered up to take her place.

As the women in the crowd stampeded for an up-close and personal look, Harry stepped inside the boutique.

Chapter Two

Four and half months later…

"Teeny Bikini Swimwear. Jacey speaking."

The words barely left Jacinta Carr's mouth when the testy voice of a creditor cut right through the line to demand past due payments on several accounts.

"I'm sorry the check I sent bounced." Jacey lowered her voice to a discreet pitch. "I took a hit for five hundred dollars in bad checks this month alone. I know that's not your problem, but—"

"Miss Carr," the creditor snipped, "we're suspending your account today unless we receive payment in full…" Etcetera, etcetera.

Crap. Jacey pulled in a calming breath, reminded them she'd sent in a partial payment as a gesture of good faith to pay what she owed, but her appeal went ignored.

"You will get your money," she promised, and ended the call. From the stack of opened mail next to the cash register, she picked up yet another invoice that was stamped *Past Due*, and read the attached notice with pressed lips.

Her credit card issuing banks were on to her. She was using their convenience checks to make payments on her other cards. Now that she was considered a credit risk, they were hiking up their interest rates to what amounted to highway robbery. She barely kept up her interest payments as it were, but she'd managed, somehow. Now this?

She closed her eyes and exhaled a tense breath. *Don't worry, Gram-Gram.* A lump of anxiety curdled in her throat. *If I lose the store, I lose the store, but I will always take care of you.*

The lease on her store's retail space was also due to expire in a couple of months. Jacey had to tough it out a little longer. She didn't need her building manager suing her for back rent, on top of everything else.

And then there was Harry. Hot, sexy Harry who, with one wicked look at her, had put her heart in lockdown and threw away the key.

She dragged her lower lip between her teeth, seeing her fiancé's teasing gray eyes in her mind, her lips longing for the burn of his dangerous kisses. Her body craved his skilled touch. A touch she wouldn't be able to hold at bay for much longer.

Her hope of bringing something to their marriage, other than a pile of debt, she feared, wasn't going to happen, either.

There was also the matter of her grandmother. Jacey's shoulders drooped. She was paying for the best care money could buy, but her grandmother wasn't getting better.

Bills were mounting and, while Harry's willingness to buy her financial freedom was tempting, she wouldn't take a dime from him. Not that she thought he would stick around once he found out—in her ex-fiancé's words—about the "baggage" she carried around with her. Or when he found out exactly how she paid the bills.

She picked up the phone, dialed his office line and, when he didn't answer, she left a message. She ached to hear his deep, whiskey-smooth voice. It was a voice she could happily drown in, a voice that did things to her body that would shock a phone sex expert.

She called his cell, and when he didn't pick up, she hung up, realizing she'd taken for granted his accessibility.

They needed to talk. There were things he needed to know. Things she couldn't seem to find the strength to tell him. He'd smile that beguiling smile of his, touch his lips to hers, stroke her arm, brush her bangs from her forehead, and any will to resist would abandon ship.

All she'd think about from that point on was peeling Harry's clothes off and giving him a tongue bath.

But…no, no, and no. No tongue baths until she told him what he should have known *before* she accepted his proposal of marriage *and* his ring.

Jacey stared at the two-carat diamond on her finger. It flashed with striking green fire, and hid a mysterious amber-colored heart. The stone drew such admiration that it scared her to admit it was the real deal. But Harrison Allandt would never settle for anything less.

That meant when the time came to tell him a few truths, she could very well lose him.

Not something she was ready for. Especially after she'd already strayed into the danger zone with him. The memory of their last dinner date—how he'd made her come using his words, the sensual thrust of his fingers easing up into her pussy—brought fresh, fiery heat to her cheeks.

They'd dined *al fresco* at the Ugly Orange, a local eatery surrounded by Hawaiian orange trees in fragrant bloom, at a private table covered with a long white tablecloth.

Over dessert—a slice of caramel drizzled, baked red-banana pie—Harry had leaned in close to her, to lick away a golden strand of liquid sugar that had dribbled from the fork, and down her chin.

He'd been as subtle as a torpedo blast about what he wanted to do to her in that booth, too. "My fingers are dying to play with your clit, *mon amour*. Please…"

She didn't shy from his hand skimming up her thigh and she parted her legs, wide…wider to grant him access to her steamy core. His heated breath fluttered down the length of her neck. She'd gasped in shocked delight as his finger flicked aside the shield of her panties, and slid between the smooth sex lips surrounding her pulsating clit.

His fingertip stroked up one moist fold of her labia, isolated her clitoris and slid around that rosy jewel in maddening circles that drenched his finger. First one, then another finger swept in just as he snaked kisses up her neck, lightly flashing his tongue along the shell of her ear…

Jacey's lips parted. She closed her eyes. Lust breached her limbs, weakened with memories of his expert fingers whose flicks and strokes had had their exquisite way with her.

She blew out a recovering breath now, anxious for a distraction from the sensations flooding her body. A shipment of goods had arrived earlier, and she desperately needed a respite from the fiery flashback that wet her panties and beaded her nipples.

On her way to the stock room, she didn't expect to run into the object of her desire. His six-foot one-inch muscled frame lounged against a garment rack with the ease of someone who'd been there a while.

"Harry!" She blinked, her heart hopping aimlessly around in her chest.

How long had he been standing there? How much of her conversation had he heard?

Though his sensual lips curved with a pleasant enough smile, his velvety gray eyes lacked their easy sparkle that always made her feel welcome. Hectically good-looking, his cotton twill slacks in eggshell white, and open-necked camp shirt the faded black of a sun-baked beach pebble flaunted his dark looks and powerful physique.

"Hello, Sin." Harry greeted her by a fragment of her name that lit a pink flame in her cheeks and sent nervous shivers trailing down her spine.

"Why do you call me that?" she whispered, her stomach twisting in dread.

"Why not? It's what I wish for. Nights of sin, with you."

His gaze prowled along her body in a lazy study. The warning flares shooting across her mind went ignored in favor of the sexy itch invading her body's secret places.

Covered from head to toe in her sapphire-blue, stretch-lace top and a matching sarong skirt that touched her ankles, her nipples crested inside her bra, aching to be objects of his desire.

Her clit pulsed against the crotch of her panty, demanding some much needed attention, too.

His gaze drifted to her eyes. "Long day, hmm?"

She nodded, unsure how much he'd heard, or what he might be thinking.

"I've come to take you to dinner, Jacinta. Steak and lobster."

"Oh." She backed up against the counter, excitement tensing up her thigh muscles as he stepped closer.

His cologne, a blend of oriental woods, suede and jasmine, combined with his rampant sexual energy, created a dynamic cocktail that lit her senses and coaxed her pussy into gushing, soppy wetness. She wanted to kiss him. Bite him. And God help her, fuck him.

He cocked a brow. "Oh?"

"I-I'd love that, Harry. Can we make it a late dinner…?"

"I was hoping, just this once, that you'd close up shop early, perhaps?" He drew her against him, tipped her face up and lowered his lips.

She welcomed the hungry probe of his tongue into her mouth with a fierce lick of hers. When his thumb sought out and found her nipple through her top, she didn't jump back. He pinched it, rolled it between his fingers, tugged gently on it, urged on by the heated sounds that whispered from her lips.

"I'm wearing you down, aren't I?" he

murmured against her lips.

Her fingers clawed into his hair. She responded with a breathless "mmm," granting him permission to carry on.

The slit of her skirt fell away as she spread her legs so he could fit himself, *jam* his lower body, in between her thighs.

With lazy ease, he bent her back against the sales counter and cradled her body in his arms. "You smell like mountain flowers, and guava, and honey…"

As his lips grazed her neck, she felt the thrust of his cock lengthen against her pelvis.

"Harry, someone could walk in any second," she cautioned, then kissed his mouth, sucked on his lower lip, and reached down to grab his ass.

"I see how worried you are." He flipped up her skirt and slid his fingers inside her panties. She gasped. Pummeled by delicious sensations, she stared up at him, her breaths coming out in ragged shots.

"So," he murmured, his fingers swimming in her pussy petals, slippery with her body's juices drenching her panties. "I haven't misread any signals at all."

The doorway sensors chimed.

He groaned, pulling his hand and body away as Jacey wriggled from his embrace.

"Hi! Hope I'm not interrupting?" quizzed a female voice.

"Hello! Come on in," Jacey invited, then turned to him. "I'm sorry, Harry," she mouthed the apology before rushing over to assist her customer.

****

While Jacey helped the petite redhead pick out several bikini styles, Harry lounged against the sales counter and plotted to pick up where they'd left off once she finished with this customer. Suddenly, another customer walked in.

"Mother hell," he swore under his breath.

Then in strolled yet another customer. All hope of getting her back in his arms anytime soon took a sudden nosedive.

He shrugged back his impatience, half tempted to buy out her merchandise just to be the center of her attention.

Nearly five months without any white-hot fucking, he had to admit, might be fraying his nerves. But the moment he saw her dancing in her store window, Harry wanted her in his life, and no one else. He'd waited this long to feel her body flame at his touch. What was another hour? Another day?

"Do you think this top is too small?"

The redhead stepped out of a dressing room and approached him, fiddling with the triangles of a stretchy tie-died fabric bursting with explosions of turquoise and red.

Rosy areolas flashed him as she tugged the bikini-top around a pair of rebellious breasts.

He looked away, only to find Jacey frowning at them.

"Sweetheart," he held her gaze, even as it occurred to him that another woman openly finding him attractive just might be a good thing for her to see. "She has a question about size…"

By the time the redhead paid for her purchases, Jacey's eyes sparked jealous green fire. He liked it, liked seeing her ruffled. It made him feel needed by his beautiful, and elusive, girlfriend.

Irked she might be, in no way did he invite *that*. It still didn't stop him from hoping that her customer's bold come-on would convince her to do something about their physical relationship. Or rather *lack* of it.

He sighed, feeling guilty at the turn his thoughts were taking. For a man who knew what he wanted, lately it seemed he wasn't so sure how to go about getting it. Leaning forward, he crossed his forearms on the counter and studied the tempting *it* in question.

His gaze ate up her face, and lingered on her soft lips, one side dimpling when she smiled over something a customer was saying to her. Dark, evergreen eyes, with amber irises that shimmered under a long fringe of toasty lashes, flicked him a teasing look that acknowledged his admiring stare.

He smiled at her, enjoying how her lips parted and her eyes widened as she stared back at him. All too soon the moment faded. She turned to answer her customer's questions, and the loss of that connection deepened the confusion swirling in his thoughts.

Without a doubt, she had a face that could turn a man's head, and the sensuous, fuck-me-please body of a…well, he had never seen Jacey naked.

Can we take it slow, Harry?

The bulge under his belt throbbed. He'd agreed to take it slow. It wasn't an unreasonable request.

Not when his no-holds-barred pursuit of her had resulted in a diamond engagement ring winking at him reassuringly on her finger, just two and a half months after they'd met.

He also traveled extensively as a diamond broker. While coming home to the hot welcome of her body was as yet a fantasy, his ring on her finger allowed him to rest easy from the threat of other males competing for her affection. Besides, her body wasn't the only reason he'd fallen in love with her.

He admired her sense of pride in owning her own business—an indication she didn't expect him to keep her entertained twenty-four seven. She stimulated him with lively conversation, shared on many levels—from local island economy to business trends, to food and wine. He also loved how her mind wasn't fixated on shopping, fashion, or dieting.

Once…he'd exercised poor judgment with a woman and had learned a pricey lesson. Jacey had restored his faith in the opposite sex with her refreshing sweetness, her strong work ethic and sense of independence. He was also able to put that cluster-fuck with Brandi behind him.

After this week, he had no intention of being away from Jacey again. At least, not without bringing her with him. He was turning his travel obligations over to a senior manager. It was high time he and Jacey took their relationship to the next level. One that, he hoped wryly, included a bed. With her in it.

"Now, about dinner…" he began, after the

redhead strolled out of the store, but not without a farewell wink at him.

"Harry, I'd love to, but I can't afford to miss the afternoon wave of shoppers that come in about this time…"

Harry checked his mounting frustration. Progress. They were making progress. His ass had delighted in the clutch of her fingers, but he had promised to take it slow.

She'd recently confided that her grandmother, whose care she was responsible for, might not be coming home from the assisted care facility as soon as she'd like. Surely that was adding to her anxiety. The furrow between her brows now struck him as worrisome, and pulled him outside of his own wants and needs.

From what he'd gleaned of her phone conversation, she might be having money problems, too. He could certainly help with that, but would she let him?

She'd turned down every offer he'd put on the table so far, and it was driving him crazy. While money wouldn't solve the intimacy issues between them, it would go a long way in giving her some peace of mind.

"Jacinta, it's been over a week since we last saw each other, then I walk in here to a phone call that has you upset—"

She looked up from the cash drawer, alarmed. "How much of that call did you hear?"

"Enough. Who do you owe money to?"

"It's not your concern—"

"*Mon amour*, what affects you, affects me. If

there is any way I can make life easier for you, I would like to know."

"That's so sweet of you, Harry, but no worries. I'll be okay. I have enough in my savings to cover all those checks."

"Honestly?"

She nodded, but would not look into his eyes.

"Then let me take you to dinner tonight. Please?"

"There is no one to mind the store if I leave early," she said pensively.

He took a deep breath, and forged on. "I've offered to give you the capital to upgrade to a more upscale locale," he reminded gently, "and to hire more staff. Your landlord is charging you top-dollar for retail space in the last rundown building left in downtown Honolulu, Jacey. I can even buy out your lease, if that's what you're worried about."

"I can't let you do that. It's important that I do this myself."

His mouth thinned. Fed up with hearing the word "can't" he asked, "Then I suppose letting me take care of you is out of the question?"

"Harry—"

"Let me guess…you can't do that either." He drummed his fingers on the sales counter and struggled to temper the ache blistering his insides.

He loved her. He was faithful to her. That nearly five months of his adult life had passed without sex was a testament to his willpower. And while his hunger for her racked his nerves, it stumped and aggravated him to know she didn't even want his money. It made him burn even more hotly for her.

He looked at her, hoping his disappointment didn't show. "Jacey, I would never interfere with your independence. I love that about you, I do. But, there are some things that a man wants do for his woman, things he can share, but you won't let me. I find that disturbing. Among other things."

He paused when the two remaining customers walked up to the counter with purchases in hand. Patiently, he waited for her to finish ringing them up.

"Are you talking about…sex?" Jacey asked when they were alone again.

"There is also that. I won't deny that I've hoped," he cleared his throat, "we could find a compromise. I haven't been able to get our last date out of my mind."

Harry swallowed now as his mind and body endured the memory of those moments in that booth, sliding his finger between her soft thighs and into her hot, wet body. He'd wanted to pleasure her. Wanted to give her something to remember him by—to accept something from him.

"You need me, Jacey," he'd murmured in her ear. "Let me give you some release."

He'd slicked his fingers up and down either side of her clit, covering them in her slippery essence so that his fingers might slide easily around her luscious bud.

Her tight canal juiced up with lust, and he'd laughed softly against her neck. "You're a little cock fountain, darling. I can't wait to be surrounded by you…"

Gently he pinned her clit between his thumb and forefinger, fondled the tiny, soaked treasure, and ate the moan that flew past her lips. "Shhh…half the valley will hear you."

"Then *stop*…"

"I *can't*. Not when your sweet pussy needs my fingers buried deep inside right now. Say yes…"

All she could do was nod.

He plunged one long finger into her tunnel, then two, kissing her mouth; savoring her tiny sounds of ecstasy meant for his ears alone.

He used his thumb to massage around her clit, but only giving the sensitive nub an occasional butterfly stroke to tantalize, to push her toward her climax.

"Harry…" she'd sighed above the sounds his fingers were making as he plunged them in and out of her pussy, "I'm about to—"

He'd kissed her mouth. She ground her hips to an erotic, sexy beat, "Come against my hand, beautiful," he'd urged, then slipped a third finger inside her, stretching her dripping, tight walls further.

He knew the moment she fired. Her lashes lowered, her body arched and her hips undulated with sensual strokes.

He had loved every second.

He'd taken her shudders and sighs of release deep into that place in his heart, reserved only for her. When she found her breath, she looked up at him, her cheeks wild and pink.

"Don't you *dare* be embarrassed."

"But what about you? I can—"

"No." He'd shaken his head. Having waited this long for her, a hand job just wasn't going to cut it. "I can wait," he'd assured her, not realizing back then, over a month ago, exactly how hard waiting for her was going to be…

The slender hand Jacey reached out and placed on his chest jogged Harry's mind back to the present. To the warning every nerve in his highly aroused body raged at him to heed. It cautioned him to stay away from her. Told him that the touch of her fingers was dangerously close to sending him up in flames, and that his self-control was about to take a flying leap out the window.

Thank you for purchasing
this Wild Rose Press, Inc. publication.
For other wonderful stories of erotic romance,
please visit our on-line bookstore at
www.thewilderroses.com.

For questions or more information
contact us at
info@thewildrosepress.com.

The Wild Rose Press, Inc.
www.thewilderroses.com